There is one m

a doozy. I really, really hope you can forgive me.

"Oh, Cassidy. What else have you done?"

To make sure you have the best possible chance at finding Tanya, I—

The cabin door suddenly opened and a man stepped inside, then stopped in apparent surprise when he saw her.

Shanna shouted and clawed for the pistol in her pocket. She started to bring it up.

The man leaped at her, tackling her to the floor.

Bam! The gun went off.

VANISHED IN THE MIST

LENA DIAZ

This book is dedicated to my fierce sisters,
Lisa Detmers and Laura Brown, for facing cancer head-on with dignity and courage. I thank God for your strength and am so grateful you're both cancer-free now. Love you so much.

ISBN-13: 978-1-335-69020-3

Vanished in the Mist

For questions and comments about the quality of this book, please contact us at CustomerService@Harlequin.com.

TM and ® are trademarks of Harlequin Enterprises ULC.

Harlequin Enterprises ULC
22 Adelaide St. West, 41st Floor
Toronto, Ontario M5H 4E3, Canada
www.Harlequin.com

Printed in Lithuania

Lena Diaz was born in Kentucky and has also lived in California, Louisiana and Florida, where she now resides with her husband and two children. Before becoming a romantic suspense author, she was a computer programmer. A Romance Writers of America Golden Heart® Award finalist, she has also won the prestigious Daphne du Maurier Award for Excellence in Mystery/Suspense. To get the latest news about Lena, please visit her website, lenadiaz.com.

Books by Lena Diaz

Harlequin Intrigue

A Mystic Lake Mystery

Hunting the Crossbow Killer
Vanished in the Mist

A Tennessee Cold Case Story

Murder on Prescott Mountain
Serial Slayer Cold Case
Shrouded in the Smokies
The Secret She Keeps
Smoky Mountains Graveyard

The Justice Seekers

Cowboy Under Fire
Agent Under Siege
Killer Conspiracy
Deadly Double-Cross

Visit the Author Profile page at Harlequin.com.

CAST OF CHARACTERS

Kaden Rafferty—Owner of an underwater salvage company, he's in the town of Mystic Lake to try to find the body of a teenager believed to have drowned in the lake.

Shanna Hudson—Expecting an uneventful vacation at her sister's cabin, this private investigator gets pulled into the case of a missing teenager along with Kaden.

Cassidy Tate—Shanna's sister is desperate to find her missing student and to help the girl's parents have closure. She lures her PI sister to town under false pretenses to get her help.

Tanya Jericho—This high school sophomore's disappearance sets into motion a dangerous, complicated investigation that puts the lives of many people in jeopardy.

The Phantom—Are the stories of this shadowy figure roaming the woods outside town a myth? Or is he a real-life bogeyman hunting for human prey?

Mystic Lake Police Department—Police Chief Beau Dawson and his small crew aren't thrilled to have civilians Kaden and Shanna interfering with their search for Tanya.

Billy Thompson—As the owner of the marina and a retired military pilot, does he know more than he's telling about what he's seen when flying over the mountains?

Chapter One

Shanna Hudson didn't believe in ghosts. She didn't believe in the boogeyman. And she certainly wasn't going to quake in fear over the so-called Phantom the locals claimed lived in the remote area of the Smoky Mountains above the town of Mystic Lake, an hour outside of Chattanooga, Tennessee. But as she stood in the late afternoon sun at the end of her sister's dock overlooking the vast lake with the same name as the town, a tingle of uneasiness skittered up her spine. Not because of the myths and legends that surrounded this place, but because of one indisputable fact.

People had died in this lake.

So many had died or disappeared over the years that Mystic Lake was officially one of the deadliest lakes in North America, second only to Georgia's Lake Lanier. Both of those lakes were deadly for the same reason: the hazards beneath their deceptively calm surfaces from when they'd been created by flood waters that submerged whole towns decades earlier.

There was one notable difference, though. Lake Lanier had been created on purpose, with the building of a dam to provide hydroelectric power and water to nearby towns. Mystic Lake's inception was an act of nature, the result of a devastating confluence of storms that permanently rerouted a small river down the side of a mountain and buried a town, drowning most of its residents.

Shanna shivered as she looked out across the dark water and wondered just how many poor souls had met their end here. And how many cars, homes and entire trees lurked in the depths today, ready to snag a boat or tangle in a swimmer's hair to add to the lake's tragic history. From what her sister, Cassidy, had told her, the townspeople did what they could to make the lake safe. Known hazards were hauled out when feasible and budgets allowed. Warning signs had been posted in particularly treacherous areas. But there was no way to eliminate all potential threats. The lake was too deep, too big. Its waters covered thousands of acres of land and extended through the foothills for miles. Yet, in spite of the dangers, both locals and tourists flocked here to boat, fish, or swim, believing the worst wouldn't happen to them.

Until it did.

In the decades since the lake had existed, not a single year had passed without at least one person dying in a mysterious boating accident or by drowning. Usually, it was a handful, sometimes even more.

She shook her head, still amazed that her sister had finally worn her down enough to get her to come here. But Cassidy's most recent request had been different. Instead of pressuring Shanna to travel to Mystic Lake in her official capacity as a private investigator, Cassidy had offered her lakeside cabin for a week's vacation while she and her husband went on a Caribbean cruise they'd won in a contest. Being teachers, it was hard to get permission to take a vacation in April, just weeks before the school year ended. But they were top performers and this was a special circumstance, so their dream trip had been approved.

Shanna was happy for both of them. They deserved this time away. And the invitation to Shanna to enjoy their cabin while they were gone had come at a time in her life when it was too tempting to pass up. The lure of escaping the mounting pressures of running her PI company, which was located in Morgantown, West Virginia, particularly after her last, exhausting case, had been too tempting to turn down. Well, that and because her ex-boyfriend was struggling to accept the *ex* status of their relationship. Maybe her being out of town for a week would help Troy come to terms with their breakup. If not, if his stalking behavior continued to escalate, she'd have to escalate her response, too, by involving the police. Again.

She patted her right pants pocket, reassuring herself that her gun was there. Not that she expected to need it. But she wasn't taking any chances, especially if Troy figured out where she'd gone and decided to make a surprise appearance. The ability to bring her gun was her sole reason for driving the nine hours rather than fly. She hadn't wanted to deal with the hassle of declaring her weapon to airport security and being forced to store it in a checked bag, where it might be *supposedly* lost.

Guilt rose inside her, crowding out her concerns about her ex. Shanna had refused her sister's many requests that she look into the disappearance of one of Cassidy's high school students almost a year ago. And yet, here she was, for purely selfish reasons. But she'd always been clear with Cassidy when turning her down. Shanna didn't have contacts in this area, no confidential informants or insider knowledge to help her solve the case. And besides that, her West Virginia PI license wasn't valid in Tennessee.

Could she have looked into the case in an unofficial civilian capacity rather than as a private investigator? Yes. Of course. But she had no reason to expect that she'd do a better job in this unfamiliar area than the local police had. Plus, there was another reason she'd turned down her sister. It was the same reason that she'd refused to come here after Cassidy first moved to Mystic Lake two years ago, when she'd gotten married.

Shanna was afraid of the water.

Not the drinking kind or the showering kind. Her fear focused on anything large, deep, or scary, including lakes, ponds and even swimming pools, like the one where she'd nearly died as a young teen. She'd sworn off ever allowing herself to be that vulnerable again by going near or in the water. And until today, she'd kept that vow.

Part of keeping it meant refusing to search for her sister's missing student, Tanya Jericho. After all, Tanya was believed to have perished in this lake a few weeks after her sophomore graduation, in May of last year. Since her body had yet to be found, she was still labeled as missing eleven months later. Investigating her disappearance would have meant spending time around the water, probably even going out on the lake in a boat. Since Cassidy knew about Shanna's fear, she never should have asked her to work the Jericho case. Although, to be fair, her younger sister might not realize just how debilitating Shanna's fear could sometimes be. Cassidy was too young to remember what had happened all those years ago. Only Shanna, her parents, her therapist, and the police knew the full terrifying truth about that day at the pool.

Squaring her shoulders, she turned her back to the water. Immediately breathing easier, she headed up the gently sloping hill to her sister's log cabin. When she'd arrived earlier, she'd parked her silver Lexus beside it, but had left her suitcase at the bottom of the porch steps. She'd wanted to deal with the lake head-on, right away, instead of allowing dread to build up. Now, if Cassidy called and asked her, she could honestly say she'd faced her fear and was fine. More or less, even though her heart was racing and her palms were sweaty. No one needed to know that part.

She smiled at the clay pots with pink and white flowers spilling over their sides that hung from the porch railings. Unsurprisingly, the cabin's foundation was also surrounded by flowers and shrubs. Her little sister and her husband both loved anything to do with nature. With it being full-on spring, they wouldn't miss an opportunity to take advantage of the mild weather to grow something. There were probably plants inside the house too with detailed instructions on how Shanna should care for them this week.

She hauled her suitcase up to the wide wooden porch that ran across the front of the cabin and used the key that Cassidy had mailed her to unlock the door. Even after having been told it was a one-bedroom, one-bathroom cabin, she was still surprised at how small it was as she stood in the opening. Her sister and her husband's high school teacher salaries meant they weren't exactly flush with cash. But they could have afforded something bigger than this. They'd probably opted to devote the bulk of their mortgage money on expensive lakefront property rather than get a larger house in town on a much smaller, more affordable, lot. The view and unspoiled location would have been too hard for them to resist.

What mattered, of course, wasn't the size of the cabin. What mattered was that Cassidy and her husband, Gavin, seemed happy. And they'd made a welcoming, cozy home here. The soaring vaulted ceiling saved the place from feeling claustrophobic even though it was probably a quarter the size of Shanna's two-story brick home in West Virginia.

True to her sister's personality, the wide open room with the sitting area to the left, the kitchen to the right with the table in the front corner near the door were all so clean they practically sparkled. The windows framed an impressive view of the lush, green Smoky Mountains. And the cabin was high enough on the hill that Shanna could focus on the Smokies, rather than the lake, when peering out those windows. It was the perfect setting for her planned week of solitude and peace. And once her sister returned, they could spend some time catching up before Shanna left for home.

The stress she'd been struggling with from her most recent case, her arguments with her ex and even her few minutes on the dock all seemed to lighten as she stepped across the threshold. It was as if she'd left her worries outside. It felt good. Really good.

She drew a deep breath, smiling as she turned and shut the door. But when she saw what was on the back of the door, the stress came hurtling back, like a fist slamming into her chest. A faded eight-by-ten piece of paper was taped to the door. Across the top, printed in large black letters was a heart-wrenching, ominous word.

MISSING

The color picture beneath the caption framed the smiling face of a young girl with long red hair and a smattering of freckles across her pale cheeks. Her bright blue eyes stared back at Shanna, making her throat tighten. This was the girl her sister had wanted her to try to find. Had Cassidy simply forgotten to take down the flyer? Or had she put it there to make Shanna feel guilty? Maybe it was worse than that. Maybe her little sister had tricked her and this wasn't a simple vacation opportunity. The couple was probably hiding in the bedroom right now, waiting to ambush her and beg her to look for this girl. No, not *this girl.* She was a real person and deserved to be thought of by her name, the name printed beneath her picture.

Tanya Jericho

She let out a shuddering breath and turned away, her good mood having completely evaporated.

"Cassidy? Are you here?" She headed to the door in the middle of the back wall and yanked it open. "Cassidy? Gavin?" She strode into the bedroom and glanced around, fully expecting one or both of them to be there. But aside from the king-size bed, with its patchwork quilt and the usual assortment of nightstands and a dresser, the room was empty. She checked the closet and surprisingly large, attached bathroom as well. Both were devoid of a sneaky sister or her equally sneaky husband.

Okay. Maybe assuming the worst about them was unfair. A faded poster of a girl who'd been missing for almost a year wasn't enough evidence to prove her sister had an ulterior motive for inviting her here. Shanna strode back into the main room of the cabin, circling the two-tiered kitchen island to get a drink of water while trying to quiet the suspicions in her mind. But when she rounded the island, what she saw on the countertop by the sink had her tensing up again: a half-inch-thick manila folder. Her sister had promised to leave a note about the local sites, hiking trails and restaurants. Nothing about the thickness of that folder had her believing that's what she'd find. Drawing a bracing breath, she took the folder to the table and flipped it open.

And swore, viciously.

She'd been tricked. Shanna didn't have to be a private investigator to reach that conclusion. It was spelled out clearly and succinctly on the very first line of the first page in the folder.

Hey, sis. I'm so sorry that I tricked you.

Shanna swore again and plopped down in one of the chairs at the table to read the rest of the note. Her sister explained that she was desperate to help the Jericho family and the only way she knew how was to ask her brilliant private-investigator sister to look into Tanya's disappearance. Cassidy begged her to please read everything in the folder, which had been given to her by the missing teen's parents. The stack of pages contained background information on their daughter, what they'd documented and collected about the investigation that the police had done, as well as their own attempts to find out what had happened.

If you read this and are still set against helping, I'll understand. You can enjoy the cabin regardless and have the vacation you deserve. I had to try one last time to get your help or I wouldn't be able to live with myself. Forgive me, please? Love you.

Shanna sighed. Of course, she'd forgive her sister…eventually. Honestly, in her place, she'd have probably done the same thing. But what Cassidy didn't seem to get was that

Shanna hadn't made her decision lightly to not investigate the girl's disappearance. She'd agonized over whether or not to come here and help. But in a town built around and dominated by a deadly lake, she'd decided it was best to trust in the local police rather than try to interject herself into the investigation.

Thankfully, her sister had given her an out, telling her it was okay to stay and use the cabin anyway. Cassidy and her husband hadn't lied. They really were on a cruise, as the note went on to explain. To do right by her sister, all Shanna had to do was read the folder. Then she could set it aside without any guilt and get on with her plan to do absolutely nothing but sleep, read and eat for the next seven days.

Her gaze, seemingly of its own accord, slid back to the picture of the young woman on the flyer.

So young. So innocent.

Shanna had been that young once, that innocent. And what had happened to her had been horrendous. But she'd survived, because of the help of some really good people. Who was helping Tanya? Who was helping her parents?

Shanna started to shake. *No.* This wasn't her problem. It wasn't Shanna's fault that this girl was missing. It wasn't her duty to help every single person who got into some kind of trouble. She was only one person. There was only so much *she* could do.

Anger came to her rescue, giving her the strength to surge to her feet and snatch the missing poster off the door. She was about to slap it on top of the stack of documents in the folder when she noticed dark shadows of words bleeding through to the front of the flyer. Someone had written on the back and she didn't have to guess who.

Cassidy.

She fisted her hands at her sides. *Ignore it. Don't turn it over. Don't read it.*

Oh, for the love of…who was she kidding? She was an investigator for a reason. Her curiosity was her superpower, driving her until she uncovered every little crumb of evidence to solve a case. Unfortunately, it was also her kryptonite. She let out a strangled groan and flipped over the flyer. Her sister's neat teacher's handwriting flowed across the page.

There is one more thing I need to tell you, and it's a doozy. I really hope you can forgive me.

"Oh, Cassidy. What else have you done?"

To make sure you have the best possible chance at finding out what happened to Tanya, I—

The cabin door suddenly opened and a man stepped inside, eyes wide with surprise as he stared at her.

Shanna clawed for the pistol in her pocket.

The man leaped at her, tackling her to the floor.

Bam! The gun went off.

Chapter Two

"Get off me!" the woman yelled, twisting and bucking beneath Kaden Rafferty as he wrestled the pistol out of her right hand.

He sent it sliding across the hardwood floor out of her reach and grabbed her now-free wrist before her fist could make contact with his jaw.

"Knock it off, all right?" he practically growled. "Obviously there's been some kind of misunderstanding here."

"Misunderstanding?" She bucked against him again, her knee nearly connecting with a vulnerable part that had him settling his full weight on her to stop her from trying that move again.

"Lady, if you'll just quit fighting me I'll let you go. You're obviously in the wrong cabin and—"

"Wrong cabin?" Her blue eyes blazed up at him, hot with anger. "You're the one in the wrong cabin. Or maybe the right one if you were hoping to break in and steal something. You just didn't expect anyone to be home."

"You're right about one thing. I was told that no one would be here."

She jerked her wrists, struggling against his hold. "Who told you that? Your partner in crime? Let me guess. He's waiting outside with a truck to load up whatever you both plan on stealing."

"Not unless my partner in crime is a high school teacher named Cassidy Tate."

The mad-as-hell brunette suddenly grew still, her brow wrinkling in confusion. "Cassidy Tate? How do you know her?"

"Remember the part where you accused me of breaking into this cabin? If you think back, instead of trying to get your gun to shoot me again—"

"I didn't shoot you."

"Not for lack of trying."

She rolled her eyes.

He prayed for patience. "I didn't kick down the door. I used a key. The one Mrs. Tate mailed to me last week when she hired me."

The woman blinked, her eyes widening. "Cassidy hired you? To do what?"

"You know her?"

"Not as well as I thought I did. She's my sister."

"Ah. That explains it."

Her eyes narrowed suspiciously. "Explains what?"

"She was stubborn and feisty on the phone, calling several times over the course of three weeks insisting that I consider her proposal. Somehow, she convinced me to help her, free of charge in exchange for lodging and food. That stubbornness must run in the family."

She swore.

He couldn't help smiling. The salty words coming out of that pretty mouth weren't the way he'd have expected this beautiful woman to speak. She was nearly as tall as he was, which put her at close to six feet. Her slim, athletic body, delicate facial features and long, thick brown hair were an appealing combination. The only things destroying her supermodel potential were her generous breasts, which were currently burning a hole in his chest. She didn't have that waiflike half-starved look that so many models had. And he most definitely approved.

She was gorgeous, especially when she wasn't trying to punch or shoot him. She'd stopped struggling and her face was turning a delightful pink. She was either still mad and planning her next attack, or she was embarrassed about something.

"Why did Cassidy call you?" She was markedly calmer now as she waited for his reply.

"She wanted me to come here to search for a missing girl."

The woman groaned. "What's the girl's name?"

"Tanya Jericho."

She squeezed her eyes shut for a moment, and her brow wrinkled as if she were in pain. Then her body went lax and soft beneath him as all the fight drained out of her. "I'm guessing you're the doozy she mentioned in her note."

"Doozy?"

"Will you please let me up? You're right. There's been a misunderstanding."

Her soft curves were starting to do alarming things to him now that she wasn't trying to kill him. He was eager to let her go before she noticed his body's response. But he wasn't even close to trusting her.

"You don't have another gun in your other pocket, do you?"

"I wish."

He smiled again. The woman was delightfully sassy.

Too bad she was so bloodthirsty. "I'll release your wrists on the count of three. Don't try to pull any sucker punches when I let go."

"Just get up already."

He chuckled and rolled off her, then leaped to his feet and swiped the pistol off the floor before she could get it.

She stood and frowned, then shrugged as if she didn't care even though she'd been clearly going for her gun.

He shoved it into his back jeans pocket, shaking his head.

"Don't look at me that way. I wasn't going to shoot you." She frowned and glanced around the cabin. "Where did that bullet end up, anyway?"

He pointed toward the wall to the right of the door. "Judging by the splintered wood, I'm guessing it's buried inside that log."

She winced. "Cassidy is going to kill me. Then again, it serves her right for this little stunt she pulled." She cleared her throat and offered her hand. "Let's start over. I'm Shanna Hudson, Cassidy's big sister."

He shook her hand. "Kaden Rafferty." He motioned over his shoulder. "I hear there are bears around here. Mind if I shut the door?"

She blinked. "Bears? Oh. Yes, please do." She sat at the table.

He shut and locked the door, then took the chair across from her.

They sat in silence for a long moment, then she let out a deep breath and picked up a piece of paper that must have fallen to the floor earlier. She turned it over and read a paragraph on the back, then set it on the table.

"What's your superpower?" she asked.

"My superpower?"

"The reason Cassidy made that deal with you, free work in exchange for food and a roof over your head. I'm a private investigator. And you are?"

"Ah. I see. She tricked both of us into coming here to investigate the case of this missing girl. But she didn't tell either of us the other one was coming. Am I getting warm?"

"Burning up."

He grinned. "Then I guess my superpower is that I own a search-and-recovery company. We operate out of Charleston, South Carolina. This is my first time coming to Mystic Lake, Tennessee."

She crossed her forearms on the table. "What type of search and recovery does your company do?"

He sat back. "It's not your turn."

"My turn?"

"To ask another question."

"This isn't a game."

His amusement fled. "No kidding. I'll be dead serious then, and tell you that almost being shot wasn't in my plans when I drove eight hours pulling an extremely expensive boat and giving up a lucrative contract to take on your sister's request pro bono."

Her eyes widened and her cheeks flushed pink again. She glanced past him, presumably at the splintered log, before she looked back at him. "I'm sorry. I truly am. We've both been played. You weren't told I'd be here. And I didn't know anything about you. I hadn't finished that part of the note that my sister left before you opened the door. I honestly thought you were an intruder and that my life was in danger. Otherwise, I'd have never drawn my gun."

The sincerity in her voice assuaged his anger and had him nodding his acceptance of her apology.

"You were going to ask me a question," she said. "Please. Go ahead."

He cleared his throat. "Yes, well. The trip here was a long one and I only stopped once, to gas up. I also drank way too much water along the way."

A bubble of laughter escaped her as she pointed toward the far wall. "Go through that door. Once inside, the bathroom's the second door on the left."

Chapter Three

When Kaden returned to the table, the beautiful brunette was deeply immersed in whatever she was reading in the folder. He sat down across from her. When she didn't look up, he asked, "It's Shanna, right?"

She started, as if she'd forgotten he was there. His ego took a hit. Not that he thought he was God's gift to women. But he'd been told he was decent-looking and being outright forgotten by a beautiful woman wasn't typical for him.

"Are you married?" He glanced at her left hand. No ring. But some people didn't wear them these days.

She blinked. "Uh, no. You?"

"Nope. No girlfriend, either, at the moment. Is there some jealous guy I need to worry about?"

Her eyebrows raised. "Why would you need to be worried?"

He motioned toward the doorway in the back wall. "There's only one bedroom in this cabin and one bed. Since we're both staying here—"

"There's a bed-and-breakfast in town. You can stay there."

"I prefer the cabin."

"You're going to the B and B. It's my sister's cabin. It wouldn't make sense for me to leave it for a stranger to use."

"Except that your sister invited me and gave me a key."

She frowned and closed the folder. "Why would you want to stay where you aren't wanted?"

"Ouch. You don't mince words, do you?"

"Not normally, no. What's the problem? Do you need money? I can pay for the B and B if that's the issue. It's not your fault that my sister, ah, overbooked her cabin." She pulled out her cell phone. "I'll even call and reserve a room for you."

He stood. "Don't bother. I won't use it." He moved to the front door.

"Wait. Where are you going?"

"To put my boat in the water. I saw a public ramp a couple of miles down the road."

"There's a ramp not far from the B and B, too. I drove around town scouting things out before I drove to the cabin. It's a decent ramp, spacious, lots of parking. Wouldn't that make more sense?"

"Not when I'm planning on tying my boat up at the dock I saw outside this cabin after I finish my work every day. I'd like to park my truck and trailer here since I'll need the truck off and on this week. I'd ask you to drive them back to the cabin for me since I'll be driving my boat. But since you're in denial, I'll hire someone else to do it." He opened the door.

She jumped up and followed him onto the porch. "Hold on a second."

He stopped and leaned against the railing.

"You said you'd come back here, after you're through with work. What's that about?"

"I would expect that's obvious. I'm going to start my

search for Tanya Jericho. There are still several hours until sunset. Might as well start now."

"Using your boat?"

"Since she allegedly disappeared either on or near the lake, yes. I'm going to search for her using my boat. *Underwater* search and recovery is my company's specialty. It's why your sister sought me out."

Something dark seemed to pass across her eyes, like a shadow. Fear? Confusion? Whatever it was, it had her silent and deep in thought.

He didn't wait. He jogged down the porch steps to his truck.

The sound of swearing told him she'd come out of her trance or whatever it was. He tried not to laugh as she ran after him. Forcing a straight face and a bored look, he turned around and leaned against the driver's door as she stopped in front of him, slightly out of breath.

"What now?" he asked.

"You haven't even read the folder. You don't know where to look."

"I'm assuming your folder is like the one that your sister sent to me. I've already read it and pinpointed the first grid area I'm going to search."

"Just like that?"

"Just like that." He opened the door and hopped into the driver's seat.

Her soft hand was suddenly on his, stopping him. "The police had divers in the water, several times. No one ever found anything."

"That's where my—what did you call it?—*superpowers* come in. I have the latest handheld sonar technology that's specifically programmed to pinpoint anything under the water that has the characteristics of a submerged body." He gently removed her hand. "I really need to get going. It'll take a while to get my boat in the water, arrange for my truck to be driven back here, drive my boat to the area I want to search, and then spend a few hours actually searching. If I don't get going soon, I won't have enough daylight left to make starting the search today worthwhile."

She moved back so he could shut the door. But as soon as he started the engine, she knocked on his window.

He sighed and rolled it down. "Now what?"

"You don't have to hire someone to drive your vehicle to the cabin. I'll do it and then you can… You can pick me up on the—the boat here at my sister's dock." She swallowed as if that hesitant statement had been hard to say. Then she added, "I'm going with you on your search."

"No. You're not."

She stared at him in confusion. "Why not?"

"Because you have something else to do."

"What would that be?"

"You were calling the B and B to try to evict me. I'm not sharing my boat if you're bent on not sharing the cabin."

"Oh, for crying out loud. That's childish."

He arched an eyebrow.

She crossed her arms, clearly struggling with her decision. She didn't seem to be afraid of him anymore. But something had her clearly worried.

After nearly a full minute of silence, he decided he'd waited long enough. "Like I said, daylight's wasting. I need to go."

Something akin to panic crossed her face as she glanced from him to the boat behind his truck. She cleared her throat and seemed to gather herself. "Okay, okay. We can share the cabin. Just give me a minute to get my purse and—"

"Another gun you probably have hidden inside? I don't think so." He revved the engine.

Her hands fisted at her sides. "You're the only one who has a gun. Mine. Which you *are* going to give back to me at some point. But right now, I need to lock up the cabin. Not that there's a lot of crime around here, but some hiker could come along and decide to help themselves to anything inside. I can't leave Cassidy's home unprotected."

He pretended to consider her statement when what he really wanted to do was laugh. She was so fun to tease. "Okay. Lock it up. Hurry." He shifted into Reverse and began to carefully back the trailer up so he could turn around.

She swore a blue streak and ran for the cabin.

Chapter Four

Shanna stood at the edge of her sister's dock watching Kaden's impressive blue-and-white boat, or maybe it was a yacht, bobbing up and down in the water as he reached his hand out to help her board.

"That's—that's a really big boat," she said, stalling. "What kind is it?"

"A Scout 530 LXF. Thirty-three-footer. Are you coming on board?"

She ignored his outstretched hand. "Do you have another life jacket? For me?"

"Of course. I'd never allow someone to go out on one of my boats without one."

"*One* of your boats? How many do you have?"

"Enough so that my company can work several contracts at a time. Otherwise, I'd never earn enough to cover expenses, let alone turn a profit." He motioned toward her. "Now, if you'll just—"

"Is it like the one you're wearing? The life jacket you have for me? That one looks awfully thin."

He glanced down at his jacket. "The thinner ones are more comfortable than the bulky ones and don't hamper movement the way those do. But they're just as buoyant. If you'll step over the side, we can—"

"Are you positive it will keep someone afloat if they fall overboard? Mystic Lake is well-known for people going under and never coming back up. There's something…odd about this lake. Something—"

"Mystical?" He smiled.

Her face warmed. "That's not what I'm saying. I just—"

"Want to be sure you're safe?"

"Right. Yes." She cleared her throat, desperately trying to calm her racing pulse. *Breathe. In, out, in, out.*

He dropped his hand. "Shanna?"

"Yes?"

"What are you afraid of? The boat? Or me?"

She blinked. "What makes you think I'm afraid?"

"It's a balmy spring day and you're shivering like it's ten below zero. You're also extremely reluctant to board even though you said you wanted to come along."

"I do. I want to help, to tell my sister I did everything I could to find Tanya. I mean, she tricked me, tricked both of us. But she must be truly desperate to have done that. There's no way I can ignore her request now and go back to my original plan. Especially when a total stranger is willing to help. I *have* to do this."

"Your original plan?"

"Do nothing. Sleep late. Ignore the world for a week."

"Got it. No shame in that. I'm sure you work hard and could use the break. Go on up to the cabin. Relax. Leave the search to me and I'll update you when I get back. I've got this." He turned away.

"Wait!"

He sighed heavily and glanced over his shoulder. "Yes?"

Her stomach knotted as she tried to ignore the sound of

the dark water lapping against the dock. "It's not the boat. And it's definitely not you."

He frowned in confusion.

"That I'm...afraid of." Her face flamed with embarrassment. "It's the water."

He blinked, understanding dawning in his expression. "You're afraid of the water, and you still want to come with me?"

The wake from a passing boat had the dock bobbing slightly. She stiffened, the traumatized teenager deep inside her desperate to turn away, to run to her sister's house and hide beneath a mountain of blankets. But the memory of the missing poster and the sound of her sister's voice pleading for help over the phone was battering her with guilt.

Please, Shanna. Tanya's parents need to bring her home. They've accepted that she's no longer with us. But they can't rest until they've given her a decent burial. Help them.

She swore beneath her breath, then stretched out her hand. "I'm ready."

He stared at her a long moment, as if weighing her resolve. Then, instead of taking her hand, he straddled the side of the boat, one foot on the dock, the other on the deck, and clasped his hands around her waist. He lifted her up and over the side so quickly that she didn't have time to be afraid or protest. He steered her into the interior behind the glass windows and had a life jacket on her almost as fast as he'd lifted her onto the boat.

She marveled at his strength, considering she was in no way tiny at five-eleven. He was probably six foot two, maybe taller, his broad shoulders and impressive biceps speaking to the strength she'd felt in those arms. That strength was reassuring, since he was the one who would be guiding the boat. Unfortunately, logic was doing nothing to stop her roiling nausea.

Deep breaths. Deep breaths. Don't look at the water.

As he adjusted the straps on her vest, she finally found her voice again.

"Thank you," she whispered.

"No worries." His deep voice resonated with empathy and understanding, sending a pleasurable tingle up her spine that had nothing to do with nausea and everything to do with how appealing he was. "You're safe. The boat's high-powered, with several engines. More than enough horsepower to get us back if an engine fails. It's sturdy, easy to maneuver. Everything you might need is down those steps in the cabin. A galley, bedroom, head."

"Head?"

He chuckled. "I'm guessing you don't speak *boat*. The head is the bathroom. The galley's the kitchen. And you can remember the overall areas of a boat by thinking of it like a compass, with north being the front. North, south, east and west are bow, stern, starboard and port."

"Got it. I think. Wait. There's a bedroom? Earlier you were arguing that we'd have to share my sister's house, implying that we'd have to share the only bedroom, too."

"Don't get me wrong. This is a hell of a boat, with all the luxuries I could possibly want. But staying on it a whole week? I prefer the freedom of movement of an actual house, at least when I'm not out on the water searching. I can certainly sleep here at night. But I'd prefer to share your sister's place during the daylight hours, if you're open to it, especially since she promised the kitchen would be stocked. I have drinks and snacks on board, but little else."

"So you were teasing earlier?"

His deep brown eyes sparkled with amusement. "I certainly wouldn't mind sharing your bedroom, and your bed, if you ever want to." He winked, making her face heat again, and her belly tighten for an entirely new reason. How could she want him when she barely knew him and felt so awful right now? "But, no," he continued. "I wasn't serious when I teased you about sleeping in your sister's cabin."

She couldn't help smiling in response and shaking her head. But even that small movement made her nausea worse. She drew several quick breaths, desperately fighting the urge to throw up.

His expression turned serious as his brow furrowed with concern. "You can lie down on the bed if you'd like. But I recommend you sit outside. There's built-in seating. It's secure. And the fresh air should help ease your nausea."

"That obvious, huh?"

"You've gone from Casper the Friendly Ghost white to Shrek green."

She laughed, then pressed a hand against her protesting stomach and desperately tried to ignore the gentle rocking motion of the boat and the sparkling of the sun off the water surrounding them.

"Sit. Once I drive us to the desired location, I'll launch off the stern to conduct my search. You won't have to do anything but relax and work on your tan."

"In jeans?"

"I didn't bring any bikinis for you. But I'm fine with you just wearing your birthday suit."

She laughed again, then groaned, her stomach protesting her every movement. "What did you mean by launch?"

Another small boat passed with two fishermen on board. They waved as they went by and Kaden waved back, then motioned toward the rear of the boat as he turned his attention back to Shanna. "The deck at the stern. That's where I'll go into the water, scuba dive."

She felt the blood drain from her face. "Oh. Okay."

"That's the underwater part of search and recovery."

She gave him a weak smile. "Earlier you mentioned sonar. I guess I figured it was built into the boat and you wouldn't need to dive."

"You're partly right. The main equipment maps out images below the water to help with navigation so I don't run aground. It also helps me locate large objects, like a submerged car. But it's not that effective with smaller objects, such as human remains. Detail work requires a diver. So does recovery, for anything we're looking for."

She winced. "Makes sense. I'm not thinking things through very well. Usually I'm better than this."

He lightly squeezed her arm. "You're facing your fears to help your sister and Tanya's family. You can't get much better than that."

She stared up at him, marveling at his patience and kindness. And how had she not realized how good-looking he was until now? He was clean-cut, with short brown hair and whiskey-brown eyes. Ruggedly handsome was the cliché that came to mind. He wasn't one of those pretty boys, the ones with a perfect tan and long lashes that graced the cover of a magazine—like her ex, Troy. Instead, Kaden seemed like an incredibly capable man, the kind who could build a fire by rubbing two twigs together in a rainstorm, build a shelter without any tools that could withstand the worst that nature could throw at him. That was far sexier than any cover model could ever be. He didn't seem much older than her, maybe thirty-two or-three. And yet, he wore the confidence of a man with far more years of experience. Kaden Rafferty was *hot.*

She shook her head in wonder. "How are you not married? Or escorting some beauty-queen girlfriend around on your arm?"

He laughed. "Beauty queen? Is that the kind of woman you think I'd be attracted to?"

"Well, yes, actually. Like attracts like, or so they say. And you're not exactly plain-looking."

A sexy smile curved his lips. "Neither are you."

She blinked, her mouth falling open and her entire body flushing with heat.

His smile widened, revealing straight white teeth and an adorable dimple in his left cheek. "Are you flirting with me, Ms. Hudson?"

If she didn't feel so bad, she'd be jumping him right now. She cleared her throat instead. "Unfortunately, Mr. Rafferty, I feel too bad to flirt right now."

He gave her a sympathetic look. "You'll feel better once you see how smooth she rides."

"She?"

"*Discovery.* The boat."

"Right." She cleared her throat. "It's a good name. For what you do, discovering lost things beneath the water. Just, ah, one more question." She pressed a hand to her throat. "If I need to throw up, where should I—"

He grabbed her hand and rushed her down the steps.

Chapter Five

Kaden glanced through the cockpit window toward the prow of the boat, where Shanna was sitting. Her complexion had been alarmingly pale when she'd emerged from the head earlier. But after brushing her teeth with one of the guest sets he kept on board, and drinking down a bottle of water, she'd regained some of her color. He'd tried to get her to lie down, no longer sure that her being outside, where she could see the water, was going to help her feel better. But she'd insisted she'd feel trapped down in the cabin and would rather face whatever was coming. Then she'd straightened her shoulders like any good soldier and marched to the prow, where she'd been ever since. Anyone looking at her would think she was enjoying herself, unless they caught a glimpse of her hands. She was clinging so tightly to the arms of her seat that her knuckles were white.

He wondered what had happened in her past to make her so afraid. Seeing her physical reactions to the lake, and the fact that she still insisted on being part of the search for Tanya, he couldn't help but be impressed that she refused to give in to her fears. Most people he'd met would have made a beeline for her sister's place rather than purposely place themselves in the position that she had. Heck, he probably would have stayed there himself if he felt physically ill near water.

Shanna was courageous and full of determination—both traits he greatly admired. It also didn't hurt that she was as beautiful, or more, as any so-called beauty queen that she'd mentioned earlier. But he had a feeling that comparison wouldn't go over well with her. So he kept that thought to himself.

A flash of white off the starboard side had him turning the wheel to port and gunning the engines to get around yet another reckless boater. That made three near misses in the last ten minutes. As soon as the danger passed, he glanced at Shanna. If she'd reacted, she wasn't showing it. He certainly didn't want to scare her any more than she already was. But it was hard to keep clear of all the wannabe captains around here who'd likely watched a required thirty-minute video on boating safety before being handed a key to a rental boat.

The lake finally began to widen, so he steered toward the middle, putting more of a buffer between him and the fools closer to shore as he passed the marina that had likely rented them those boats.

He'd researched this area before driving here. From what he'd learned, the main tourist season would start in the summer, about two months from now. But obviously, the people out on the river, or fishing from the shore, or just plain drinking and partying on the docks, didn't care which season it was. They were enjoying the mild weather and didn't appear to be worried about the stories—both real and imagined—of all the accidents and disappearances on Mystic Lake. Heck, knowing human nature, the mysteries surrounding this place likely increased tourism instead of putting a damper on it.

If he'd realized this many people would be out here, and how reckless they'd be, he'd have brought a smaller boat so he wouldn't have to struggle to get this one's thirty-three-foot length clear when a speedboat got too close. Thankfully, where he was headed was a much more shallow section of the lake that was less frequented by boaters. Just a few more turns and he'd be away from the crowd, assuming at least some of his online research was reliable.

He made the first turn, relieved to see a noticeable drop in the numbers of other boaters, just as he'd hoped. Still, he kept in the middle of the channel and watched for the crazies and drunks. When he made a second turn, the lake opened up, and was much wider and calmer with no other boats around. There were houses here and there tucked up in the trees along both shores. But most of the docks were empty, devoid of partiers and tourists. Most likely these homes belonged to locals and weren't being rented out to sightseers. Those locals were most likely finishing up their day at work or even preparing to make the long trek home from neighboring Chattanooga. That should make the search much safer, at least for a little while, which was always his primary concern. There were a lot of potential dangers on the water and under the water, in Mystic Lake more than most.

He slowed to four knots and checked the depth-meter gauge. Back by the marina, it had read close to fifty feet. Here, it was reading twelve. But every once in a while it would bump down to four or five for several seconds before going back in the twelve-foot range. Variations in the bottom of the lake bed were to be expected. But jumps that sharp and fast indicated something else, likely debris beneath the surface.

It wasn't unexpected, given the lake's history. There could be trees, automobiles, even crumbling buildings down there, all of which made the dangers significantly higher than one of his usual trips. He'd have to be extremely careful, not just to protect his investment in the *Discovery*, but to look out for Shanna. He didn't want to add any trauma on top of what she was already experiencing by involving her in a boating accident.

The GPS meter showed he was close to his destination, the area where Tanya had told her parents she was going to sit and read at some picnic benches under the trees at the lakeshore the day she disappeared. Looking at the bank off to starboard, he could understand why the bookish, smart sophomore, who was said to be a loner, would choose that area. It was serene and beautiful, dotted with purple and yellow wildflowers this time of year, with a dozen picnic benches scattered under the trees. The road that led here ended off to the right, a dead end. This was where access to the lake ended by land.

The closest house he could see was a good hundred yards away, high up the mountain. Still, if she'd been his daughter, he'd have been uneasy knowing she was out here all alone. Not because of the myths and legends, but because of the very real dangers to young girls—*other people*, especially men. The same things that attracted Tanya to this area could attract those who were up to no good. The kind of men who might stumble across a lone female and suddenly become her worst nightmare.

He cut all but one of the four engines. Hopefully, what had happened to Tanya was much more benign. It would be far better if she'd simply drowned, although that was tragic in itself. But to learn she'd been taken by some stranger and likely had awful things done to her before being killed would be a much worse fate. He couldn't even begin to imagine the agony a parent would feel learning something like that. It might be kinder for them to never know what had happened rather than to have the worst confirmed.

"Is something wrong with the boat? I think most of those massive engines off the back have quit running."

He glanced to port, where Shanna was standing in the cockpit opening, clinging to the nearest railing. He offered her a reassuring smile.

"I cut most of the power. The water near that bank off to our starboard side, to our right, is our destination. I'll use one engine to turn into the current while I drop anchor so we don't run into the shallows."

She looked confused, but nodded as if she understood. He wondered if she'd ever been on a boat before. If not, her fear of the water wasn't because of a boating accident. Something else must have happened.

"We got here sooner than I expected," she said. "I thought it would take a lot longer."

"It would have by car. From what I saw on the maps I studied, the main road from town winds around these mountains quite a bit. By water it's straighter, much shorter. Even going slower than a car, a boat would beat them every time out here." He checked his depth gauge again, making sure they were clear of underwater hazards before slipping past her to take care of the anchor.

Once he was back at the helm, Shanna stood beside him, shaking her head in wonder. "I had no idea they made boats this fancy and sophisticated. All of these huge screens and digital instruments look like something out of a sci-fi movie. One that has leather seats and white oak cabinetry everywhere. If I didn't hate the water, I'd probably want something just like this."

"Thanks. I think. She's a stunner for sure, quite the investment in my company. The luxurious features are a bonus, especially when we end up on an extended salvage operation. But it's the horsepower, reliability and generous-sized scuba deck that sold me on her."

"Scuba. You mentioned that before. Are you going to dive right here and search for—for signs of Tanya, assuming she went into the water as the police believe?"

"Yes and no. I won't actually dive unless my scanner indicates a potential hit."

She leaned past him, eyeing the twenty-four-inch Garmin navigation screen. "Scanner? You have cameras to see underwater?"

"Not a typical camera, no. Unless you're in the Bahamas or some other tropical paradise, where the water is crystal clear, you won't be able to see more than a few feet or a few yards. A camera doesn't do you much good under those conditions. *Discovery*'s scanners use sonar, like a bat, and draw a picture on the screen that's similar to a topographical map."

"The kind that shows how high or low land is, like mountain elevations?"

"Exactly that, yes. The instrumentation, including the depth-meter gauge, is sophisticated enough to give a pretty good picture—more or less—of what is at the bottom. Specifically, obstacles, hazards and, if we look in the right place, the item we're searching for."

"Like cars or boats? Is that what you search for most of the time?"

"Those make up a lot of our contracts. But we also get contracted for plenty of other things, like mapping out bodies of water to look for potential hazards to be removed before opening up for water traffic. We've discovered old cemeteries too, from the 1800s, as one example, that the government was forced to dig up and restore somewhere else, and have assisted treasure hunters by eliminating some areas from their searches. The list goes on and on."

"Basically, if anyone needs any mysteries figured out under water, you're the go-to guy."

He smiled. "Go-to company, at least. We're building quite the reputation, which is why your sister zeroed in on us after she went searching the internet for help."

"You haven't mentioned searching for bodies."

"We don't typically do that. But we do come upon them from time to time. It's unavoidable when locating vehicles that went off bridges, for example. That special sonar I mentioned before is what I'll use today to try to locate Tanya. Give me a minute to change and I'll show you." He headed down into the cabin and a few minutes later emerged in a pair of dark blue swim trunks.

Shanna's eyes widened as she took in his change of clothing. His naked chest in particular seemed to hold her attention. When her roaming gaze finally met his, her cheeks flushed a light pink. She cleared her throat and quickly looked away, clearly embarrassed to have been caught staring. Since her staring seemed appreciative and admiring, he didn't mind one bit. It was good to know that she wasn't completely immune to him, especially since he was definitely not immune to her.

"So what's this scanner thing you said you would show me?" she asked. "Or was that a pickup line?"

He grinned. "If it was, did it work?"

For the first time in far too long, she smiled, a true smile that actually reached her deep blue eyes. "The change of clothes worked far better than the scanner line."

If her face got any redder she'd look sunburned. But she didn't back down from her statement or turn away.

He laughed when what he really wanted to do was kiss her. But this wasn't a date. And he didn't want to risk making her uncomfortable if he was misreading her signals. She was already uncomfortable enough on the water. Worrying about a man she'd only just met making a pass at her wasn't a burden he wanted to add to her already full plate.

"The scanner, the sonar, is out here." He stepped around her and headed to the stern, crouching to pop open one of the built-in storage bins. He grabbed a towel, then pulled out the lime-green container that resembled the kind of box that might house a drill. But this was far better and more complicated than any power tool. He opened it and took out the rectangular green-and-white device, holding it up by the long handle attached to the bottom.

Shanna frowned as she stood beside him. "It looks like a computer tablet with a handle."

"That's pretty much what it is, except that it's waterproof. Shanna Hudson, meet my newest and by far coolest toy, AquaEye."

"Aqua what?"

"AquaEye. It's a handheld sonar device made by a company called VodaSafe. But what makes it so special isn't the sonar alone, it's the amazing software that goes with it. This piece of equipment is the main reason your sister asked me to come here."

"She researched search-and-recovery companies and picked you because you have a handheld sonar?"

"Pretty much. Let's say that someone drives their car off a bridge, like I mentioned earlier. Law-enforcement rescue divers go in and try to find the driver and save them. Of course, by the time they get there it's normally a recovery, not an attempt at rescue. But that's what they do. They take the body. My company is left to pull the car out. But finding the car in the first place isn't always as simple as going into the water where the vehicle was believed to have gone. A vehicle can end up being a long distance from where it went in, depending on the depth, currents and obstacles, or lack of them. In some cases someone might have last been seen driving their car and no one even knows they ended up in the water. The police might call us in that situation to search lakes and ponds near major roadways to see if the car went into any of them. Either way, my company locates the vehicle and then works to tow it out of the water."

"But Tanya didn't have a car. And she didn't take either of her parents' cars. So why does that handheld thing make a difference here?"

"This handheld device makes a world of difference because it's specifically programmed to look for sonar signatures that could indicate human remains."

"No way."

"Way. It's cutting-edge. When I heard about it, I got one for us to beta test. I'm not in the business to find human bodies. But there are many times when we locate a vehicle for the police and expect a body to be inside but don't find one. All we typically can do at that point is give the coordinates of the vehicle to the law-enforcement divers so they can perform the search for the person who went into the water with it. Once their part is done and the body is recovered, again, we recover the vehicle. After so many experiences like that, I was frustrated at always having to pull back and wait for law enforcement to stumble around trying to locate the victim. It can be a long, slow process, taking days or even weeks. I wanted to be more proactive and provide better information to them so they could find the remains more quickly."

"How would my sister have known about this…sonar device, and have asked you to come here to search for Tanya?"

He tapped the AquaEye. "The local news in Charleston did a story about this equipment and highlighted my company as a beta tester. That's why we came up in online searches when your sister was trying to get someone to help here at Mystic Lake. This sonar, and its unique programming, just might give us a chance to bring Tanya's remains home so her family can finally have closure."

She shook her head, her eyes full of wonder as she looked up at him. "A hottie with heart. Imagine that."

He almost choked, then cleared his throat. "Can't say I've ever been called that before."

"Trust me. You have. Just not to your face."

"You must be feeling a lot better. You're smiling again."

She sobered and glanced around, making him regret saying anything. She had a beautiful smile and he hated seeing that haunted look in her eyes.

"I almost forgot we were on the water," she whispered.

He gently tilted her face up toward him. "I'm sorry that I reminded you." In spite of his best intentions, he couldn't resist temptation anymore. He took a chance that he was reading her right and pressed a quick kiss against her forehead. "I'm not the only hottie around here." He winked.

She let out a burst of laughter, then covered her mouth.

Relief swept through him. He'd read her right. And he was glad to have gotten her to laugh again. And glad that she hadn't slapped him for kissing her, even if it wasn't on the lips. He was starting to look forward to returning to her sister's place later. Spending some time with this interesting, beautiful woman in close quarters wouldn't exactly be a hardship. And maybe sometime soon he could give her a real kiss instead of a peck on the forehead. But returning to the cabin wouldn't happen until he finished his work here, so he'd better get to it.

After shrugging into his life jacket again, he opened the starboard-side panel near the rear of the boat to give him access to jump into the water.

"Wait," Shanna called out, her eyes dark and shadowed again as she clung to the railing beside the opening, surprisingly close to the water in spite of her fears. "You're going into the water without a tank and wetsuit and whatever else?"

"I'm not planning on diving just yet. I'm going to swim around at the surface and hold the sonar just below the water to see if it pinpoints any areas I need to search more thoroughly. If it gets a potential hit, that's when I'll get my scuba gear. I honestly don't expect any hits right away. It's been almost a year since her disappearance. Her body, if she went into the lake around here, could have moved quite some distance due to the currents. That's why I perform grid searches. I start at the last known location, or in this case, the last suspected location. Then I spread out from there, tracking on my maps where I've searched and where I still need to search."

"Makes sense. But…if you're swimming, and you need help, I can't… I don't know how to…"

"You can't swim?"

She shook her head. "No. I mean yes. But I haven't, not in a long time. And, honestly, even if I needed to, I don't know that I could. I'd probably drown because the panic would make me freeze." Her cheeks flushed red. "I'm really sorry. I'm not much help out here."

He lightly squeezed her hand. "No apologies. You're doing great. I'm the one who should apologize. When you insisted on coming along I automatically assumed you could swim, or that you could in spite of your anxieties. I should have asked to be sure." He glanced at her life jacket, reassuring himself that it was still secured the way it should be.

"I wanted to come. That's on me. But I wasn't thinking about being your wing man if something happened. I should have been more upfront."

"Don't worry about me," he told her. "The life jacket will save me, if I need saving. All you need to do is sit there and wait."

"But if something does happen—"

"It won't."

"But if it does—"

"Then you'll call nine-one-one. If your phone doesn't have service out here, you can call from the hard-wired satellite phone in the console, beside those fancy screens I showed you earlier. That's it. Nothing else. Promise me you won't go into the water, no matter what."

She looked past him, her face going pale again. "Trust

me. I won't." She made her way to one of the seats and sat down. She was holding on so tightly, he could see her knuckles turning white again. "Okay. I'm ready."

He almost decided then and there to cancel the trip, to bring her back to the cabin and return on his own tomorrow. But he'd already seen how stubborn she could be. She'd probably hate him for it. Besides, she'd gone through self-torture just making this trip. She'd likely not forgive him if he didn't at least try to find Tanya after she'd ridden all the way out here.

With one last reassuring smile, he slid into the lake. He treaded water, using his legs to kick just enough to keep his head up. He clutched the sonar device in his right hand and held it slightly below the surface, scanning back and forth. His first scan was toward shore. When he held up the device to look at the screen, it was clear. No hits. He turned and submerged the device again, sweeping it left and right. Then he lifted it out of the water to look at the screen. This time, it showed an *X*. He stared at it in surprise. Was it malfunctioning? He truly hadn't expected any hits in this first grid. But he had to rule it out before moving to another area.

As Shanna had said, the police had searched this part of the lake last spring when Tanya was reported missing. They hadn't found anything. He hadn't expected to, either. If the sonar really was picking up human remains, then maybe her body had been pinned by some underwater hazards that the divers hadn't risked searching. That was the only thing that he could think of to explain it still being in this area after so long. Still, that seemed unlikely. Even cars, as large and heavy as they were, usually scraped along the bottom, pushed by currents, ending up surprisingly far away in most cases than where they'd gone into the water. Tanya had been missing since mid-May, nearly a year ago. How could she be right here where she'd first been reported missing? Unless this wasn't where she'd originally gone into the water.

"Is everything okay?" Shanna called out.

He gave her a reassuring nod. "Just double-checking the equipment," he called back, before submerging the scanner and trying again. When he pulled it back up, the *X* was still there. Something was beneath the surface, about eight feet down. Could it be a tree branch, or rocks, throwing off the sonar? It was still new, still being tested out. But whatever the device was picking up, it was too close to ignore. He had to check it out. And he didn't need his scuba gear to head down eight feet for a quick look. He did, however, need to take off his life jacket or he wouldn't be able to submerge.

He quickly took it off and instead strapped the AquaEye to it so he wouldn't lose it.

"Kaden, what are you doing?" Panic gave Shanna's voice a sharp edge. "Put your life jacket on."

"Be right back," he called out, figuring the quicker he got this over with the faster he could reassure her. Then he drew a deep breath and dove beneath the surface.

The water was darker, murkier than he'd expected, with visibility incredibly limited. He immediately regretted his decision to dive without first getting his equipment, which would have included an underwater flashlight. But he was already at the bottom, so he made the best of it, feeling around to see what might have tripped up the sonar.

Something slimy brushed against his hand. He jerked to the side and squinted in the cloudy water, but didn't see the fish or plant that he assumed he'd touched. The water was so gloomy and dark. It seemed to weigh him down, pressing against his chest, making his lungs burn for air far sooner than they should have. He could normally hold his breath for a good two minutes, even longer if he absolutely had do. He'd been an avid swimmer and diver since he was a kid. But something about this lake seemed…different. Even when he'd been driving his boat through the water, it had seemed as if he was moving through thick sludge in spite of the lake not appearing to be polluted or muddy. He'd definitely had to push the engines more than he'd anticipated. It was almost as if the lake was a living thing that resented his intrusion and was fighting against him.

He shook his head in disgust. The fanciful stories he'd read online about this place were messing with his headspace. He needed to focus, find whatever the sonar had seen down here before he was forced to surface for air.

He sifted his hands through the muck on the bottom, digging through rocks and sticks, pieces of wood. The bottom truly was littered with debris, the kind that could easily catch a swimmer's long hair or loose clothing and add them to the long list of others who'd disappeared in this water.

And if he didn't surface soon, he'd become one of those statistics.

His hand touched another piece of wood. It was hard, unyielding and mired in sticks and muck, just like everything else in this area. He tugged it loose and decided to bring it up to gain a better understanding of the kinds of debris he'd need to be aware of while diving in this lake.

Seconds later, blessed cool spring air rushed into his aching lungs. He bobbed on the surface, treading water, his arms and legs feeling heavy and weighted down. It was the oddest feeling, as if something was trying to suck him back under.

"Kaden! Over here."

He turned, surprised to see Shanna waving at him from the boat a considerable distance away, at least three times the distance from where he'd gone into the water. And there wasn't even much of a current to have pushed him that far.

"Kaden, grab your life jacket. There!" She pointed.

He turned again, to see it floating a few yards away, the sonar device still attached. He lunged for it, grabbing it and holding on. The strange weakness in his limbs was disconcerting and made no sense. It took all his strength to hold on to the jacket and kick toward the boat.

As soon as he reached it, he let out a shaky breath and tossed the life jacket and muck from the lake bed onto the deck.

Shanna's face was pale. He must have scared her by being gone longer than he'd intended. He really should have suited up and gone in with a flashlight and tank. With her fear of the water, it hadn't been fair to leave her alone. From the way she was shaking, he must have terrified her.

"I'm so sorry I worried you." He pulled himself onto the deck. The moment his legs cleared the water, the strange lethargy evaporated. "How long was I under?" He stood and closed the opening before turning around.

Shanna wasn't looking at him. Her body was shaking as she stared down at the bundle of debris and muck he'd tossed onto the boat. Except that it wasn't just debris.

It was a human hand.

Chapter Six

Shanna wrapped her arms around her waist as she sat at a picnic table a good thirty feet from the shoreline, watching the activity on the lake. The police had told Kaden yesterday that it was too late in the afternoon to begin their search of the lake where he'd made that horrific discovery. So they'd all agreed to meet out here this morning.

Neither Kaden nor she had been interested in dinner yesterday, so he'd stayed on his boat to do whatever maintenance boaters did after going boating. He'd spent the night there while Shanna had slept at her sister's cabin. This morning, the two of them had shared a quick, lean breakfast of toast and juice in spite of the kitchen being well-stocked as Cassidy had promised. Neither of them had gotten their appetite back yet. Then he'd left in his boat and she'd left in her car, both of them ending up at the same spot. This place, where he'd discovered that awful, severed hand yesterday afternoon.

There weren't any local police divers, so rather than wait for the state police to arrive with their dive team, Kaden had volunteered to begin the process of recovering the remains. As he dived yet again, this time in scuba gear, three Mystic Lake police officers, including the chief, assisted from their much smaller boat, holding a rope tied to Kaden and tugging it now and then. In answer, Kaden was supposed to tug back so they knew he wasn't in trouble.

She shivered as he disappeared beneath the water for the dozenth time. At least he had people with him to help if he ran into trouble. The only thing that Shanna could have done the previous afternoon was to call 911 if she felt he needed help. If he really had been in trouble, he'd have likely ended up drowning since there was nothing she could have done to save him. She felt so danged useless, frozen on that boat staring at the water and counting down the seconds since he'd disappeared beneath the surface. She'd wanted to dive in, to look for him. But she couldn't seem to move, no matter how hard she'd tried. Fear had held her in place.

Four minutes.

She would have sworn an oath that Kaden had been underwater for four minutes when he'd made that dive without any diving equipment. She'd been on the verge of making that 911 call when he'd finally surfaced. Later, he'd assured her that he couldn't have been down that long. He'd have run out of air. But she'd checked the time on her phone throughout his dive. It had definitely been four minutes. Or, at least, her phone told her it had. Maybe yet another of the anomalies around this allegedly cursed lake was that it somehow messed with electronics. It was either that, or divine intervention had protected him.

She shook her head at her fanciful thoughts, torn between her being determined to wait until all of the bones were recovered, so they could officially confirm that it was Tanya, and wanting to head back home. One thing was for certain. She wasn't ever going out on that lake again. The largest, deepest body of water she ever planned to get close to in the future was a bathtub.

"Hey, there," a friendly voice said as one of the female police officers sat beside her at the picnic table. "How are you holding up?"

Shanna gave her a weak smile. "Okay, I guess. I'm sorry, I forgot—"

"My name? I wouldn't expect you to remember. We only spoke briefly when all of us met up here a couple of hours ago to start the search. I'm Officer Grace O'Brien. That's Chief Dawson and Officers Ortiz and Collier on the boat out there. And you're the private detective that Cassidy has been hounding to come here for quite some time."

Shanna winced. "Guilty as charged."

The policewoman surprised her by pressing Shanna's hand in camaraderie. "Try not to feel guilty. There's no evidence that Tanya Jericho's disappearance was anything sinister that needed your expertise as an investigator. You should feel proud today, proud that you and Mr. Rafferty are likely bringing closure to the Jericho family by bringing Tanya home. Or, at least, helping them accept that she's truly gone so they can lay her to rest."

Shanna nodded her thanks, but guilt was riding her hard. She doubted it would go away until or unless she could confirm that her refusal to help before now hadn't contributed to whatever had happened to Tanya, and whatever the young woman may have suffered.

She watched as Kaden handed a dark plastic bag to one of the officers on the police boat. Then he dived beneath the water yet again. "You really think it's her? Tanya?"

"You don't?"

"I hope it is. Not that I want her to really be...gone. But

if it's not her, that means we still don't know what happened, where she is. Her family won't get that closure you mentioned. And someone else's family is going to get some really bad news."

"We don't have anyone else missing, at least not recently. And no one's ever been reported missing in this section of the lake. An unfortunate number of swimmers and boaters do go unaccounted for around here, more than in most lakes—"

"Second only to Lake Lanier, which is allegedly haunted."

O'Brien nodded, her expression solemn. "You've done your homework. Despite our regrettable statistics overall, we've had a pretty good run this past year. The last known person to go missing was Tanya Jericho, last spring. So unless someone else went missing and no one reported them, those remains are hers."

"There was still some tissue on the bones that I saw. If it is her, wouldn't the remains be completely skeletonized by now?"

O'Brien narrowed her eyes, as if taking her first close look at Shanna and trying to figure something out. "You seem awfully nervous about the recovery of that body. I thought as a private investigator that you'd have seen dead bodies before. But the questions you're asking make it seem otherwise. Which is it?"

"I've seen a few bodies in my line of work, more than I'd like. That's not why I'm nervous."

The officer waited, but Shanna wasn't about to discuss her embarrassing fear of water with a woman she'd just met. Or her ridiculous concern for Kaden, a man she'd also only just met, even though it already seemed as if she'd known him for years. Or maybe it was that after being so worried about him yesterday when he'd been underwater so long she felt vested in his safety and far more concerned than made sense, given their short acquaintance.

"I'll take your silence as a reminder to mind my own business." O'Brien smiled. "Not the first time I've been told that. Instead, I'll answer your earlier question. With my background from having been an FBI special agent, I can tell you that while bodies in the water do usually decompose quickly, that's not always the case. In special circumstances, it can take much longer, from a few weeks up to a year or even longer. There are a variety of factors, like temperatures, whether they were clothed when they went into the water, marine-life activity. Around here, I'm learning there's also the Mystic Lake factor to consider. The water is…different than most lakes. It's almost like it's…thicker. We've had champion swimmers tell us that swimming out here is really challenging, that the water seems to weigh you down. Whatever it is that makes it unique could potentially impact the decomposition, likely due to the currents and different chemicals and other elements that make the water the way it is."

"Thicker?"

O'Brien nodded. "That's the word we hear the most. It's a better explanation than to say there are unknown forces at play, like the lake itself is sinister in some way. So we lump all of that together and call it the Mystic Lake factor."

"Doesn't sound very scientific for someone who used to work for the FBI."

"Yes, well, things change once you've been here for a while. Or, I should say, this place changes you."

"How long have you been here?"

"Well, Alannah, my daughter, is five months old. Aidan

and I were married a year before I got pregnant and I was here several months prior to that. I guess it's getting close to three years. Longer than I'd realized. But even though I'm a transplant, I became indoctrinated pretty quickly from the day I arrived, working on a case for the FBI. I've learned quite a bit about the myths, rumors and downright lies made up about this place to know what's what."

"So you don't give credence to the legends?"

O'Brien gave her a sharp look, then looked out at the water. "I didn't say that."

Kaden popped up on the surface close to the police boat and handed another black bag to police chief, Beau Dawson.

"How long will it take your coroner—or medical examiner, I guess, in the state of Tennessee—to conduct the autopsy and confirm the victim's identity?"

The policewoman sighed. "Unfortunately, Mystic Lake doesn't have a medical examiner. We'll have to transport the remains to Chattanooga for an autopsy. A drowning victim who's been under water for a year or more isn't likely to come up high on their priority list. If they've got a caseload queued up, it might be several days."

"What about the Jerichos? If they hear about a body being found—"

"Already taken care of. Officer Fletcher—Liza—is over there now, letting them know what's going on. Since you and Mr. Rafferty located the remains while searching for Tanya, Liza is telling them that you're here looking into the case. I hope that's okay."

"Yes, of course. I should have spoken to them already. But I didn't expect..." She motioned toward the water. "This. Not so quickly, anyway. I was going to call and arrange a meeting later today, introduce myself. But this happened yesterday late in the day and…" She shook her head.

As they both watched, Kaden disappeared back underwater. Shanna looked away, too unsettled by what was happening out on the lake to keep watching. O'Brien glanced at her curiously, but didn't pry.

About twenty minutes later, the whine of boat engines had Shanna looking up again. "Looks like they're done. Kaden's boat is heading down river. But he's on the police boat, in his regular clothes again, coming here."

O'Brien nodded "Officer Ortiz is likely piloting Mr. Rafferty's boat to the marina, or wherever Rafferty wants it docked. The chief will need formal statements from you and Rafferty, which is probably why he's on the boat with Dawson and Collier heading to shore. Are you going to give him a ride to the station, or should I?"

"I've got my car. He can ride with me."

"Okay, thanks. I'll ask Liza to pick up Ortiz and Collier once they have both of the boats docked and bring them to the station. I'll meet you there." O'Brien headed toward the lake.

As the boat got closer, Shanna noticed the piles of dark bags at one end. How tragic that a person's entire life was now condensed down to those sad little bags.

A minute later, the boat idled up near the water's edge. Dawson and Kaden took turns hopping over the side of the idling boat onto the grass.

With them off the boat, the last officer, Collier, turned it and took off in the direction that Ortiz had gone with Kaden's boat.

Chief Dawson stopped to talk to O'Brien a short distance away. Kaden, his hair wet and disheveled, headed toward

Shanna. His face was grim as he looked down at her, as if trying to figure out the best way to tell her what he'd found.

"It's Tanya, isn't it?" she asked, already nodding.

His jaw tightened. "No. The… What I found down there wasn't Tanya Jericho. There wasn't much left, not enough to make an ID. But Chief Dawson was certain the pelvis bones were that of a male. Even if he's wrong, judging by the length of the femur and the tibia, the victim was at least ten inches taller than the missing teen."

Disappointment had her shoulders slumping. "I suppose it would have been a miracle to find her on our first try. You said as much earlier. It makes sense that it's not her. If it was, I'd have expected the police to have found her when she originally went missing. After all, you discovered that body really close to the area where her parents thought she'd gone that day. Do the police have any idea who he might be? Officer O'Brien didn't seem to know about any missing-persons reports that might account for another accidental drowning out here."

"Whoever he is, there's more to his death than an accidental drowning. That hand I found didn't detach from the rest of the skeleton on its own. There were tool marks on the bones."

Shanna stared at him with growing dread. "Are you saying that someone…cut off his hand?"

He gave her a tight nod. "Hopefully the autopsy will tell us that it happened after he died. Regardless, drowning victims don't have their skeletons chopped up. This guy, whoever he is, was murdered. Which begs the question of—"

"Whether Tanya was murdered, too."

Chapter Seven

Following Officer Grace O'Brien, Chief Beau Dawson, and Shanna into the Mystic Lake police station, Kaden paused just inside. If it wasn't for the gold letters above the glass door he'd just come through, he wouldn't have known this building housed the police. He certainly hadn't realized it when he'd arrived in town yesterday, admiring the row of quaint shops fronting the cobblestone street out front that bordered the lake. His assumption was that this was the tourist-focused part of town and that the government offices and other businesses were clustered somewhere else.

"Not what you expected?" Shanna's words echoed his thoughts.

"I suppose it's got everything a police department needs. A set of holding cells to the right, vending machines and the chief's office to the left. A glass-walled conference room along the back wall. The small cluster of four desks here in the squad room. It's just so—"

"Small?"

He smiled. "My Realtor sister would call it cozy. Only four officers plus the chief to take care of the entire town seems like it would be a struggle. Then again, I haven't seen that many people since arriving. I wonder what the population is in Mystic Lake."

The chief, obviously having heard them since he was only a few feet away talking to O'Brien, seemed amused as he joined them. O'Brien headed into the conference room.

"Less than two thousand locals," he said. "A third of those only live here part-time, in vacation and hunting cabins high up in the mountains. Two to three officers per thousand is usually enough in a small town like this, where the crime rate is low. But I wouldn't mind having a few more permanent officers to help when we get a flood of tourists during the summer months. We make up the difference by contracting with other law-enforcement agencies to temporarily beef up our staff during the busy times, or to help cover us when our staff takes vacations. Which reminds me, we don't have a contract with you for your services. But we'll definitely reimburse you for what you did for us today. Send me the bill."

Kaden nodded his thanks.

The chief studied him for a moment. "You don't plan on billing me, do you?"

"No reason to. I knew what I was in for when I agreed to come here at Cassidy Tate's request. I'm covering the cost of this trip, searching for Tanya Jericho pro bono. I just wish it was her we'd found today."

Dawson nodded. "Tanya's an only child. Her family's been through hell. I'd like nothing more than to bring their daughter home. But thanks to you, we'll at least have answers for another family, once we figure out who you found. On the way here, I sweet-talked the Chattanooga medical examiner to put a rush on trying to ID the remains once we transport them. But as you can imagine, with no personal effects or even clothing to help with the identification, it's going to be hard to figure out the identity of our John Doe.

None of our locals have gone missing, so it's likely a tourist who went swimming or fell off a boat and never came back up. Unfortunately, we get some of those cases most years and rarely recover a body."

Shanna addressed the chief. "How will you determine the victim's identity with mostly bones to rely on? DNA?"

Chief Dawson shook his head. "Unlikely. At least, not initially. I imagine we can extract DNA from the bone marrow, or even some of the hair that was found with the skull. But unless the victim had a reason to have his DNA in one of our national databases, that won't be how we figure out who he is. Dental records, same story. Unless we have something to compare to, they won't help us ID anyone early on in the investigation. It will require old-fashioned door-to-door knock-and-talks to see if anyone in town has a friend or relative they don't see or hear from often and don't even realize could be missing. They can check, see if they can contact him. If not, we'll add that name to a list to research. Hopefully, if the guy's not a local and went swimming on his own without anyone knowing, he'll be listed in a missing-persons report in a neighboring county. The medical examiner will give us information like height, race, age range. It will likely take quite a bit of time, unfortunately, to figure out his identity."

The sad look on Shanna's face had Kaden wondering how she dealt with investigating other disappearances without it crushing her spirit. Maybe those weren't the types of cases she was normally involved in.

As if noticing her sadness as well, the chief added, "Don't give up hope. We're only getting started. Chattanooga PD has agreed to send over some forensic divers tomorrow morning to sift the lake bed near where the remains were found. They might find a wallet or a phone, something to help us figure out who this guy might be."

He motioned toward the glass-walled conference room where O'Brien was waiting. "If you two are ready to give your formal statements about what happened yesterday, that will help get things rolling."

Kaden motioned for Shanna to precede him.

Instead, she looked up at Dawson. "May I assume some quid pro quo? Once we provide statements, can you help us by handing over anything you have on Tanya Jericho's investigation?"

His eyebrows raised but he nodded. "I'll get one of our officers to print out everything we can share."

"We need the whole—"

He held up a hand to stop her. "Ms. Hudson, there are some things that I can't turn over. Not a lot, nothing that will impede your investigation. But there are a few details we'll keep confidential to help us rule out false confessions in the future, in the unlikely event that her disappearance was sinister in nature."

She blinked. "So you have considered it could be murder. I'm surprised to hear that. Cassidy said your office dismissed the possibility."

"And I'm trusting you not to tell her otherwise." Dawson's face was grim. "You make a living as an investigator. As does Mr. Rafferty, to an extent. You should both understand how important it is not to muddy the investigative waters. We're considering everything in Ms. Jericho's disappearance. But we don't want rumors to spread and hurt her family, or our investigation. Telling your sister, who is extremely close to the Jericho family, isn't a good idea. Are we clear?"

She hesitated, then nodded. “Clear.”

“Then I’ll get Officer Ortiz to make those copies.”

Just as he spoke, the door opened and officers Ortiz, Collier and Fletcher stepped inside. Ortiz stopped, his gaze shifting back and forth suspiciously. “Why is everyone staring at me?”

“I’ve got an opportunity for you,” the chief said.

Ortiz groaned and Collier laughed.

“Thank you, Collier,” the chief said. “You just volunteered to transport the remains to the medical examiner. They’re stored in a body bag in the back of my police SUV.” He tossed his keys to a very unhappy looking Officer Collier. “Might as well take care of it right now.”

“Yes, sir,” he grumbled, as he turned and headed out the door.

The third officer, Liz Fletcher, didn’t say a word. Instead, she headed into the conference room to wait with O’Brien.

“Smart woman,” Dawson said. “Ortiz, you could learn from Fletcher’s example.”

Ortiz smiled good-naturedly. “I’m sure I could, sir.” He handed a set of keys to Kaden. “Your incredible yacht is parked at the Tate cabin, as you requested. If this lake wasn’t landlocked, I swear I’d have taken off to unknown destinations with her. She’s amazing.”

Kaden pocketed the keys. “She’s a working boat, not a yacht. But I can take your subtle hint. I’ll offer you a ride before I head back to South Carolina.”

“Was I subtle? I sure didn’t mean to be.” Ortiz laughed. “Go ahead, Chief. Hit me with my so-called opportunity.”

Kaden pressed his hand against the small of Shanna’s back and loudly whispered, “This is *our* opportunity, to make an escape before he realizes we're the reason for his assignment."

She smiled and hurried with him toward the conference room while Ortiz's shoulders slumped at what the chief was telling him.

Chapter Eight

Kaden was surprised to see that the sun was already setting by the time that Shanna parked her car beside his truck at the cabin. But recovery work always seemed to take longer than expected. Diving was something he truly enjoyed, in spite of the grim reason for it today. And time seemed to fly whenever he was in the water. Add to that the interviews at the police station, and the day was essentially over.

"You coming?" Shanna paused in front of the car.

He hopped out, then looked down the hill toward the dock. He was relieved to see his boat solidly tied where Officer Ortiz had told him it would be. Ortiz had even hung the bumpers over the side to keep the boat from getting damaged from rubbing against the dock.

"It *is* a beautiful boat," Shanna said, following the direction of his gaze. "Even though I never want to get on it again."

"Want to talk about it?"

"Your boat?"

"The reason you're afraid of the water."

"Nope."

Disappointment shot through him. He respected her desire for privacy. But he also knew burdens were easier to bear when they were shared.

When he realized she was carrying the box of police file copies that Ortiz had given them, he took it from her.

"I can carry that," she insisted.

"My mama taught be better."

She smiled. "I'll bet I'd like your mom."

"I know you would. You're a lot alike. Smart, funny and beautiful."

"Are you flirting with me, Mr. Rafferty?" she teased, echoing his earlier question to her on his boat.

"Just making an observation," he replied.

Her laughter was a light tinkling sound that sent a frisson of pleasure straight to his groin. He enjoyed everything about her. But the logical part of him kept sending up warning bells. When this week was over, they'd both go their separate ways. They had to. Their entire lives and careers were based in two completely different parts of the country. He had no desire to leave his business in South Carolina to head to…where had she said her business was? West Virginia? He imagined she wouldn't want to pull up roots and start over in Charleston, either. And he didn't get the vibe that she was the type to engage in a fling without a commitment. Which meant he needed to keep a tight rein on the wicked attraction searing his veins every time she smiled, laughed, or impressed the hell out of him with her bravery and intelligence.

Once inside the cabin, he set the box on the kitchen table, then made sure to lock the door. When he turned around, Shanna was standing a few feet away with her hands on her hips.

"That reminds me." She nodded toward the lock he'd just turned. "It's high time you gave me back my gun. It's not just bears I need to be concerned about around here. There's a killer on the loose." She held out her hand.

"Do you honestly think I would have gone into the police station with a gun?"

She considered that question, then slowly lowered her hand. "I guess not. And it's not like you'd have had it on you when you were diving."

"It's on the boat. I'll go get it."

She put her hand on his arm, stopping him as he reached for the lock. That hand was soft and warm. And if he didn't stop thinking like that he'd never survive the remainder of the week, not without a lot of cold showers.

"Keep it," she said. "You plan on continuing to sleep on the boat, right? You'll need protection."

He unlocked the door. "It's your gun. As long as you don't plan on trying to shoot me again, I'll return it. Lock the door behind me. I've got my key." He headed outside.

An hour later, they'd both finished another light dinner, this time sandwiches they'd made in the well-stocked kitchen. After cleaning up, they sat at the table with both of their case folders, as well as what the police had given them today.

Kaden motioned toward the stacks of papers and photographs. "That's a lot of dots to connect. How can you possibly perform the investigation in a week? Less, since this is day two and it's almost over. Maybe you should leave it to the police and let me finish searching the areas of the lake most likely to produce results. If you try to make heads or tails of all of this, you won't have any time left for your planned vacation."

She sighed. "You're right. I can pretty much kiss my vacation goodbye. But I couldn't give up on the investigation now, not after seeing Tanya's pictures and reading just a few of the interviews. I'm already emotionally invested. I'll do what I can until Cassidy and Gavin return. After that, I have no choice but to return to West Virginia. We have other cases my investigators are working on and I'll need to review those and brainstorm additional avenues to explore. It might be another month before I can come back. But I'm determined to see this through to the end, whatever it takes and however long it takes."

"I would think a PI would make a point of not getting emotionally invested in their work. That could lead to a lot of heartbreak, and a heck of a lot of stress above and beyond the norm."

She shrugged. "I try not to. Most of my investigations are financial in nature—follow the money. Or the usual husband-and-wife-cheating-on-each-other scenario and someone wanting evidence for the divorce hearing. Those don't bother me. But when the person at the heart of the investigation is completely innocent, like Tanya, a sophomore in high school, it's pretty impossible not to get caught up in the emotions around that. Especially empathy for the loved ones left behind. It takes its toll. That's why I don't take those cases very often." She held up her hands as if in surrender. "I appreciate the advice. But it's already too late on this one. I'm all in." She cocked her head, studying him. "It can't be easy for you either, finding what you found. And then helping the police to recover…the rest."

"That was a first, for sure. Usually law enforcement wants to immediately take over the recovery process if there's a person involved. Can't say that I want to do ever do that again."

She crossed her arms on top of the table in one of the

few spots not covered with papers. "But you still plan on continuing? Searching for another victim… Tanya?"

He arched an eyebrow. "I'm already invested."

She smiled. "Touché."

"Besides, spending more time with you will more than make up for whatever else I go through."

"Ha. I'll poll you in a few days to see whether you still feel that way. I've been told I can be way too bossy and too aggressive. Although the person who most often told me that used a much less polite word."

"Mind if I ask who that person was?"

Her posture stiffened.

"Forget I asked," he said. "None of my business."

Her gorgeous blue eyes stared into his. "Actually, it is your business. I mean, I hope it doesn't really impact you, but if you do plan on continuing to work with me—"

"I do. I can't go near the crime scene tomorrow since the police divers will be there. And it won't take long to sweep that section of the river once I'm allowed access again. Might as well spend my extra time helping you, if I can."

She nodded, looking grateful. "Then you need to be aware of a potential…complication. The person I've had a lot of troubles with—"

"Who thinks you're too aggressive?"

"Yes. His name is Troy Warren. My ex-boyfriend. We dated for only a couple of months. The warning signs were there from day one. But my hormones convinced me to ignore the red flags."

He chuckled. "Good-looking guy, I take it?"

"I thought so. But it only took a few weeks for his ugly to come out. He's…controlling, to put it mildly. Called me all the time. Texted nonstop. Got jealous when I went out with friends, regardless of whether they were male or female. Kept showing up at my office to check on me."

Kaden could feel his inner caveman wanting to come out, to find this Troy and give him a lesson on how to treat a woman. He reached across the table and took her hand in his. "Did he hurt you, Shanna?"

She stared at their joined hands, then gently pulled her hand back. "Only once. I had him arrested, filed a restraining order. That was the day I broke up with him, obviously. As so many do, though, he's largely ignored the order. I had him arrested just a week before I came here because he kept texting, calling and showing up outside my house. He made bail and disappeared. Haven't heard from him since. Honestly, the silence, not knowing where he is, has me more jumpy than when he was openly harassing me. Which is why I felt I should warn you. I don't know if his violence would escalate beyond what happened, given the chance. But since you're around me you should be careful, just in case he does show up here. I'll text you his picture."

"Is that why you brought your gun?"

"It definitely factored into my decision."

He wanted to reassure her that he'd protect her. But it was a catch-22. Although they clicked together as if they'd been friends a long time, the truth was that they didn't know each other all that well. Acting as if he wanted to be her bodyguard at this point could make him seem like the controlling one, like the ex she'd fled. Making her uncomfortable around him was the last thing he wanted to do. Which meant the next time he was tempted to take her hand in his, or even kiss her forehead as he'd done earlier, he'd have to quash those desires. She was coming off a bad relationship and didn't need to worry that he was coming on to her. That, and their lives being based so far apart meant one thing. Shanna was off-limits. He knew it. But his heart, not to mention the rest of his body, was going to take some convincing.

Her gaze searched his. "I'm sorry. That was a lot to lay on you. If you want to head back to Charleston now and leave all of this to me, I totally get it."

He was shaking his head before she finished speaking. "You haven't managed to chase me away just yet. And both of us have businesses to get back to. A week is all we've got. Let's make the most of it and see if we can figure out what happened to Tanya. Her parents deserve to know." He motioned toward the ominous stacks of paperwork. "My investigations are completely different than the type you do. You're the lead here. How do we start?"

"Thank you, Kaden. Thanks for your support, especially even after you're aware of the potential danger." This time she was the one who reached across the table and took his hand in hers.

A spark of desire shot straight through him. But he did his best to keep any sign of that from his expression. "Of course. We're in this together. For a few more days, anyway."

She pulled her hand back. "I'll check with the police back home tomorrow to see if they've located Troy yet. At least if they have, that's one less thing to worry about."

"You mean besides a killer being in Mystic Lake, a killer whose identity we have no clue about? Let alone the identity of his victim?"

"Right. Besides that. Heck of a vacation, huh?"

"At least it won't be boring."

They both laughed and she began scooting some of the

piles of papers to the side. Then she retrieved a yellow legal pad and pen for him from the brown leather satchel she'd set beside the table earlier, after they'd finished eating. For herself, she pulled out a laptop and set it in front of her.

He motioned toward the legal pad and computer. "If that's what you brought when you were planning to do nothing, you need some serious coaching on how to relax away from work."

"My satchel of supplies and my computer are my security blankets. I always take them with me. Always be prepared, right?"

"Are you quoting the Boy Scouts to me?"

She blinked, then grinned. "I guess I am. It's a good motto."

He laughed and nodded his agreement.

She picked up one of the larger stacks of papers and set it in the middle. "This is the official copy of Tanya's investigation file from the police. On most of my investigations, like the divorce cases, I have the luxury of time on my side. But we don't here, so we'll have to take some substantial shortcuts and hope we don't miss anything. Where I'd usually try to start the investigation pretty much from scratch, not relying on someone else's work, on this one we'll need to rely a lot on the foundation the police built. We'll note any inconsistencies or holes that will need more follow-up. But we can't start from nothing and hope to make enough headway to make a difference fast. I'll need you to be my devil's advocate, the person to question everything I do so you can help me see any gaps."

"Makes sense. But I'm at a disadvantage. I read everything your sister sent and used that to formulate a plan of where I'd scan the lake. I'm not sure what to do aside from that. Do we go talk to Tanya's family? Her friends at school? Try to get a better timeline of what happened the day she disappeared?"

"All of that, to an extent. But, again, we have to take some shortcuts. The police investigation, at least initially, would have been focused more on quick action to find someone they believed could still be alive. That's very different from what we're doing now, trying to find a body."

She swallowed, obviously feeling sad about Tanya, then continued. "We're more in the cold-case phase of the investigation and need to look at it that way. We'll build on what was done, and try to narrow everything down as much as possible to see who we actually need to reinterview, so as to cause the least distress to the family."

"Officer Fletcher mentioned she'd notified Tanya's family that we're looking into her disappearance," he reminded her. "Do you still want to talk to them?"

"Probably. But let's review the reports from all of their previous interviews to be sure it's necessary. I'd rather not bother them if we don't have to. Let's organize everything into piles that are logically related. All interview reports can go in one stack. Any physical evidence reports, like logs of what may have been seen or taken from Tanya's bedroom, her school locker, anything the police may have collected from the outdoor area where we were today, let's stack those together. Photographs should go in a separate stack too. Once we get all of the information sorted, we can go through each group together."

"And after we do that? What's next?"

"Normally, interviews and reinterviews. Then, I'd dive into cell-phone records, the missing person's computer, a health-tracking device if they wore one to see if we could get location data from it. Really, any technological devices associated with the missing person to help formulate who they've been talking to, what was going on in their life at the time they went missing and where they might last have been. I'd also look for a journal, or diary. Those can be a gold mine of information about daily activities and people the missing person has been interacting with, people her parents might not even know about. Many young girls keep diaries or journals without their parents ever knowing."

She powered up her computer.

He chuckled. "Doesn't sound intimidating at all. I'm sure if we don't take time to eat or sleep, we can get it done."

"Right? I know it's a lot. And that's not even all that I want to do on Tanya's case. We'll have to prioritize, decide what we think we can accomplish versus what we'll have to set aside. At least for now." She tapped her computer keys, presumably entering a password. "I definitely want to research her social-media accounts looking for anything suspicious, maybe someone bothering her online, or references she made, posts, telling us her plans in the weeks and days leading up to when she went missing so we can establish a solid timeline. I'd love to check any forensics reports too, see what the police may have found that Cassidy and Tanya's parents don't know about. But we're going to do all that as one step, or as few steps as possible. I don't want to overwhelm you, so I'll stop right there."

"Too late. I'm totally overwhelmed. I wouldn't have thought of half of that on my own. The main thing I wanted to know when I started my own research before coming here was whether she could swim, and whether she was the type to get near the water."

Her eyebrows raised. "Those are exactly the sorts of questions we need to explore. You might have more of an instinct for this sort of work than you realized."

"Doubtful. I'm just the kind of guy always focused on water. That's my job."

She shivered. "I'm grateful there are people like you to do that. I sure couldn't. Looks like we're a good pair. Our skills complement each other's. Maybe we'll get lucky and solve this together. But we honestly won't have a chance if the police didn't do a lot of the important groundwork—like cell-phone records and forensic searches of her cell phone and other technology. That stuff takes a lot of time. If our base of information from them *is* solid, and if we build an accurate timeline, then our work should point us to where we should search. If it all goes back to the lake, then it's on you to find her remains. But if this isn't a simple drowning in a place that likes to keep its bodies and hold on to them, then it could be something else entirely."

"Murder. Possibly connected with the body we found."

"That's a leap I wouldn't normally consider this early in an investigation. But, yes. I think we have to explore that as a potential theory as part of our short-cuts."

He sat silent for a moment, taking it all in. "Then we need to look into our John Doe. Search for connections between him and Tanya. Right?"

"Absolutely." Glancing at the dark windows that formed the corner of the cabin where the table was positioned, she asked, "What time do you normally turn in for the night?"

If he hadn't cautioned himself about trying to quash his burning attraction for her, he'd make some lame sexy joke in answer to that question. But he had to focus. Keep the personal stuff out of this.

No matter how much he longed to make it far more personal and a hell of a lot more intimate.

He checked the dive watch that he always wore, and winced. "It's a lot later than I realized. But it doesn't matter. I'm keyed up and won't be able to sleep anytime soon. If you're okay staying up for a while, count me in."

"I was hoping you'd say that." She moved half of the stacks of paper toward him and pulled the others closer to her. "We'll get as much done as we can tonight. Then, tomorrow, be prepared to get going really early."

"Where to?"

"The scene of the crime."

Chapter Nine

Shanna shook her head in exasperation and shifted on the picnic bench to make herself more comfortable. “I can’t believe there are, what, twenty-five, thirty rubberneckers out here at the scene of the crime? You’d think the police would rope off the entire area to keep people from potentially interfering as the divers search for evidence and more remains this morning.”

“Isn’t a rubbernecker someone who slows traffic because they’re gawking at a car-accident on the side of the road?” Kaden asked, from his seat beside her.

“I’m pretty sure it applies to anyone who’s being nosy, watching some event that has nothing to do with them and getting in the way. Not that they can see all that much, anyway, with all the mist on the lake this morning.”

He chuckled. “The mist is already clearing. As to the audience, the police officers are watching the crowd, just like us. I’m sure they’ll make sure no one interferes.” He pointed to her laptop screen, which displayed pictures she’d uploaded from the police investigation folder last night. “Having so many curious onlookers out here is a blessing in disguise. I’ve already identified five of them by comparing them to those pictures. Most appear to know each other, probably locals. I’ll do what I can to get pictures without being obvious. If John Doe's killer is out here watching the recovery like you think he might be, we should come out of here with his picture. If nothing else, it might help the police with their investigation. And if the same person did something to Tanya, it can helps ours too. Win-win."

"Are you always this happy at nine o'clock in the morning?" she griped.

"Are you always this grumpy?"

She cursed beneath her breath, making him laugh.

"Oh, got another one." He wrote a name on his legal pad.

She glanced at it. "Jessica DeWalt. Wait. Isn't she the head cheerleader from the local high school?"

"*Was* the head cheerleader. She graduated the same school year that Tanya went missing. There are several graduates from last year's senior class here, all of whom were interviewed by the police last spring. The odd thing is that they're not mingling together. They're standing or sitting around in different areas. It's a small town, even smaller school. You'd think they'd all know each other, wouldn't you?"

"Probably." She glanced around at the other picnic tables scattered around the sloped hill above the lake where the Chattanooga police divers were searching. After a few minutes of casually looking, she nodded. "You're right. It's as if they're purposely avoiding each other. You saw the football team's quarterback over there, right? By that tree? He and the cheerleader would have to know each other."

"Sam Morton. Maybe they didn't like each other at school. That could explain it."

"Maybe." She opened a new document on her computer and made some notes before pulling up the pictures again.

"Give me your list. I'll focus on trying to ID everyone while you subtly take more photographs."

"You got it." He held his phone in one hand while he made scrolling motions with the other, as if he was surfing the internet. But every now and then he'd zoom in on someone and take their picture.

"Are you sure you haven't done this kind of work before?" she asked. "You're pretty good at it."

"If that's a job offer, I'm not sure you can afford me."

She laughed, then sobered as a diver surfaced and motioned for one of the forensics guys on the dive boat to take something from him. "I think they found another bone."

Kaden nodded as he snapped a picture in their direction, then pulled up the photograph and zoomed in. "Wait. That's not a bone. That's—"

"A steel rod. Like the kind they implant in bones when they've been shattered. Which means—"

"They'll be able to trace it."

"Or we can." She minimized the photos and typed in the address for the Mystic Lake High School website.

He hovered over her shoulder, watching the screen.

"Take pictures," she reminded him. "We need to identify all the onlookers." She blinked, then looked up at him. "I'm being bossy and aggressive, aren't I?"

He slowly shook his head. "No. You're being the boss, as you should be. You're heading the investigation. I'm your helper. Forget what Troy told you. Those are monikers insecure jerks put on women to try to make themselves feel more superior. Don't let him get to you."

Her eyes actually started tearing up. "Remind me again why some lucky woman hasn't snapped you up as a husband yet?"

He opened his mouth as if to respond, then seemed to think better of it and simply shrugged.

Her face heated. She'd expected one of his flirty replies. Maybe she was making more of the attraction between them than there really was. Or maybe the attraction was mainly on her side and he was just the kind of guy who was nice and made you feel good about yourself, without meaning anything deeper by it. She cleared her throat and started typing again. "We need more pictures. Please."

"Peyton Holloway."

"What?"

He held up his phone, showing the photograph he'd just snapped. "Prom queen. Another recently graduated senior. Most of the people out here this morning are older, the retiree type who can check out what's going on without worrying about missing work. Sure is odd that the younger ones watching the recovery of a body in the lake are mostly kids from Tanya's school. You'd think they'd be at college, or working right now."

Shanna swiped through several more screens on the school website. "Here's the one I was looking for. Tristan Cargill."

He set his phone on the picnic table and looked over her shoulder again. "Another senior who graduated last year. I haven't seen him here. Why did you bring up his photograph?"

"I remembered reading his interview, the opening discussion where the police make small talk to establish rapport. He was in a boating accident several months before graduation, shattered his left leg. He was in a wheelchair for a while but was walking with a cane when it was time to head down the aisle to get his diploma."

"Shattered his leg?" Kaden took his phone and zoomed

in on the picture he'd taken of the diver handing what he'd found to a forensics tech. "It might be long enough to stabilize a femur. Or a tibia. But I sure hope our John Doe isn't another teenager."

"Preaching to the choir."

Neither of them spoke for a while. They sat quietly, openly watching the flurry of activity taking place on the lake. When the news came, in the form of Officer O'Brien hurrying over to them as she put her cell phone away, it was no surprise to learn that their John Doe had been identified, by following up on the serial number on the steel rod.

It was Tristan Cargill.

"What are the odds?" O'Brien said. "A local high-school kid is found murdered in the same area where another missing high-school kid is believed to have disappeared? I don't think Jericho's disappearance should be treated as a potential drowning anymore."

"I agree," Shanna said. "Although it still might be, it's not much of a leap to think the two could be connected."

O'Brien looked around. "Everyone here is a local. If the killer came back to visit the scene of his crime today, he's no stranger. He's one of us." Her eyes took on a haunted look. "And if Tanya was killed, murdered, and it's the same perpetrator, we may have another serial killer on our hands. We may be looking for more bodies."

"Another serial killer?" Kaden glanced at Shanna. "You don't seem surprised to hear that there's already an active serial killer in this area."

"That's because he's not active. That case is closed. My sister told me about it."

"That's right," O'Brien said. "The killer, well, he's not a threat to anyone anymore. And that all happened long before Tristan Cargill was killed." She looked around at the curious faces turned their way, then lowered her voice. "I hope no one else heard that. I need to perform the notification before Tristan's family finds out from someone else." She started to turn away, then paused. "We'll obviously be actively working on Tanya's disappearance again to see if there's a link between these two cases. I recommend that you both back down, go home. If the killer knows you're looking into any deaths for which he's responsible, it could be dangerous for you. Cassidy will understand you stopping your search." Without waiting for a reply, she hurried toward her police SUV, which was parked where the road ended.

Shanna began furiously typing on her computer.

Kaden sighed. "You don't plan on stopping, do you?"

"Nope."

"I didn't think so. Guess I'll hang around, too, to keep you out of trouble."

She rolled her eyes and continued typing.

"What are you doing there?" he asked.

"Jumping to conclusions and letting my theory lead me instead of the evidence."

"Isn't that what we're not supposed to do?"

She stopped typing. "Yes. We're short-cutting, remember? Seeing where we can go with what we have. Two teens from the same school in a tiny town go missing or are murdered within days, weeks, or months of each other depending on the medical examiner's conclusions about Tristan Cargill's time of death. We'd be idiots for not thinking they could be related. O'Brien thinks the same thing. You heard her."

"She's also part of the same police force that hasn't found

Tanya and wouldn't have found John Doe on their own. Emulating them and jumping to conclusions doesn't sound like the right way to go here, at least not based on your earlier cautions."

Her face heated. "I hate having my own words thrown back at me."

"Then you're really not going to like this. I have a theory too."

"Okay. What is it?"

"We already discussed how odd it was that so many of the school's recently graduated seniors were out here. What if the killer is one of them?"

She glanced around, a chill going down her spine. "I couldn't even begin to pick one of them as a suspect. They're all so young, innocent looking. But it's not like killers go around with an M tattooed on their foreheads so we can pick them out."

"That would make it too easy," he teased, then motioned behind her. "Maybe we can do one of those shortcuts you mentioned and talk to someone who likely knew all the other teens, including Tanya and Tristan."

She glanced over her shoulder. A young brunette was standing off on her own by a thick oak tree, her hand to her throat as she watched the divers at the lake.

"The prom queen," Shanna whispered. "The most popular girl in school. She had to know both of our victims."

"Looks like she's leaving."

"Watch my laptop." Shanna jumped up and hurried after the departing girl.

Chapter Ten

"This was a bad idea." Kaden shifted on his feet and leaned against the porch railing of Cassidy Tate's cabin. "We're wasting time we could be spending following other potential leads while waiting for a prom queen who isn't going to show."

"Her name is Peyton Holloway. She'll show."

"What makes you so sure?"

"Because of the deal I made with her by the lake. She was extremely agitated to be seen talking to me after I was seen talking to the police. I left her alone only after she promised to come here."

"And you believed her?"

"Since I warned her that I'd pressure the police to bring her in for questioning if she didn't, yeah, I'm pretty sure she'll be here."

"Brutal." He grinned.

"Whatever works. As nervous as she was it seems as if she may know something. I just hope it's a lead that will take us to Tanya."

He straightened away from the railing. "Looks like we're about to find out. That's the blue Mazda she drove earlier coming up your driveway."

Shanna looked past him. "Score."

The sedan seemed like a toy as it pulled up beside Kaden's huge black Ford F-250 truck. He turned back toward the cabin. "I'll get us some drinks. As pale as she is, looks like she'll need one. Or two."

"No alcohol," Shanna warned. "She's not legal."

"Well, I need one." He headed inside.

A few minutes later, a very nervous young woman was sitting on the edge of one of the recliners in the Tate cabin's main room with Shanna and Kaden sitting across from her on the couch. But other than saying hello, she'd barely spoken.

"Ms. Holloway," Kaden said. "Would you feel less nervous about answering questions if I leave?" He started to get up, but she waved him back down.

She drew a shaky breath. "I'm sorry. It's just… I guess I'm in shock. When I heard that policewoman say they'd found Tristan, I—I couldn't believe it. I didn't even know he was missing."

When she didn't continue, Shanna asked, "Why were you so afraid to speak to us back by the lake?"

Her dark brown eyes widened in surprise. "I wasn't afraid. I just didn't want to. You have no idea what the police put us through after Jericho went missing. I'd rather avoid that again if I can. The reason I agreed to speak to you is because you're Mrs. Tate's sister. She did a lot for me in school. I probably wouldn't have graduated without her help."

"She'll be happy to hear about your appreciation. You said the police put 'us' through a lot. Who did you mean by 'us'?"

"Um, you know. Us kids, from school. I swear the cops

grilled everyone who'd ever passed Jericho in a hallway to see if we knew anything. It was ridiculous."

"Jericho. Is that how the kids referred to her at school?"

"Huh? No. I mean… I don't know. I didn't even know her. We never associated with each other. Not once."

"Her name is Tanya."

"Sure. Okay. What did you want to ask me?"

Kaden sat back against the couch and crossed his arms. He didn't want to assume anything about Peyton just because she was one of the popular kids at school. But the way she was referring to Tanya, as if she was beneath her, tended to confirm the clichés rather than dispel them. He couldn't help wondering whether Tanya was bullied by some of the popular kids, maybe even Peyton Holloway.

"You said you didn't know that Tristan was missing. Since you used his first name, can I assume he was a friend?"

"He is…was."

"But you didn't know he was missing."

"Well, no. But, I mean, since graduation a lot of us kind of…went our own way, you know? It's what people do."

"You graduated last May?"

"Yeah. Almost a year ago." She shook her head. "Wow. Time flies."

"When is the last time you saw Tristan? Or heard from him?"

She chewed her lip a moment. "I guess…it would have been at the graduation after-party." Her knuckles whitened as she clasped her hands together.

"I'm sorry, Peyton," Shanna said. "I understand the events at the lake were quite a shock. But I need to understand the lay of the land around here, being an outsider and all. My sister, Mrs. Tate, wanted me to look into Tanya's disappearance and I'm hoping you can help by answering our questions."

Peyton chewed her bottom lip. "How did he die?"

"The cause of death will have to be determined by a medical examiner."

Her hands fisted in frustration. "What do you want from me?"

Kaden gave her a reassuring smile. "I'm sure you're a busy woman and we appreciate your time. Ms. Hudson and I are trying to locate Tanya Jericho to help give her parents closure. You were one of the key leaders at school, from what we've heard. So we're hoping you can tell us what you know about Tanya."

As he'd hoped, hearing him call her a leader had her puffing up with self-importance. "Yes, well, I had some influence, for sure. But like I said, that girl—Tanya—wasn't one of us. I mean, wasn't in my circle of friends. I doubt I can really tell you anything about her."

"What about Tristan Cargill?" Shanna asked. "Did he go swimming in that area a lot? Or boating?"

"No. Never. That's not an area where we, I mean he, would ever hang out. Wrong side of town, you know?"

"No. I don't know. Can you explain it to me?"

Peyton let out an impatient breath. "That's not one of the nicer parts of the lake. And it's dangerous, with steep drop-offs. My friends and I hung out in the more, you know, exclusive areas."

"Then why were you and so many of your high-school classmates out in that area today?"

"The same reason everyone else was. To see what was

going on. You hear lots of police sirens and stuff, you go look. It's a small town."

"Okay, I get that. You said you didn't hang around Tanya. What about Tristan? Did he?"

She made a derisive sound. "You know he's rich, right? I mean, his parents are rich. They have homes all over the country and only come here in the cooler months. For the most part, Tristan has always lived here alone. Well, except before he turned eighteen they always had a housekeeper. I mean, it's not like his parents could leave a minor unsupervised for months, right? Anyway, no. Tristan never hung with Jericho, I mean Tanya, either. You know, the more I think about it, the more I think that cop I heard by the lake was wrong. The body they found must be Tanya. There's no reason for Tristan to have even been there. He's on his gap year."

"Gap year?" Shanna asked. "Like when someone skips a year after high school before starting college?"

"Exactly. Wish I could have done that but my parents would never go for it. He was due to head off to Europe a few weeks after graduation. That's the last I heard about him." She clasped her hands tightly again and looked down at the floor.

Kaden exchanged a knowing look with Shanna. Peyton Holloway was hiding something. The question was whether it had anything to do with Tristan's disappearance, or Tanya's. Or neither. Nothing she was sharing seemed like anything they could base an investigation upon. Then again, he wasn't the PI. Maybe Shanna was getting more out of this than he was.

Shanna continued to press for more details, but the

young woman wasn't very forthcoming. Then Shanna suddenly threw Peyton a curve.

"When was the last time you saw Tanya?"

Peyton stiffened in her chair. "Tanya? I don't...like I said. We weren't friends. It's not like we hung out together. Ever. Look, I've answered your questions even though I don't know anything." She stood. "It's getting late. I need to go."

Shanna checked her phone as she too stood. "It's only lunchtime. You have an appointment?"

"Appointment. Right. Yes. I have to, ah, be somewhere."

"Of course. Sorry to have kept you. Thank you for helping."

"Helping?"

"With our investigation into Tanya's disappearance."

"Oh. Right. Sure." Peyton couldn't seem to get to the door fast enough, pulling it firmly closed behind her as if to ensure that Shanna wouldn't follow her.

Shanna turned around at the door. "I screwed that up."

Kaden crossed to her. "What do you mean?"

"Without being obvious, look past me through the windows. She's on the phone, isn't she?"

"She's backing out but, yeah, looks like she's talking to someone. Hands-free phone, I'm guessing."

Shanna swore. "She's hiding something. And now, she's telling whoever else knows her secret that we're on to them. I should have been more careful, not gone full bulldog on her trying to rattle her. It could have been more helpful to have a bug in her car before she called whoever she's speaking to now. We might have learned quite a bit."

"You're talking about planting a listening device in her car? Isn't that illegal?"

"Not if I got approval from law enforcement as part of the murder investigation. I should have talked to the chief before pressing so hard."

"I don't think we've learned anything useful enough to convince the police to get a warrant. Or did I miss something?"

She headed into the main part of the kitchen area. "How much did you drink before I came inside with Peyton?"

"I was kidding earlier. I didn't get anything."

"Perfect. Are you willing to be our designated driver today?"

"You do know it's not even one in the afternoon, right?"

She grabbed a beer from the refrigerator. "I'll take that as a yes." She opened the bottle and took a deep sip. When she set it on the countertop, Kaden leaned on the raised part of the counter across from her.

"What did you learn from that interview?" he asked.

"That depends."

"On?"

"On whether Tristan Cargill went missing before or after Tanya."

He stared at her a long moment. "You suspect Tristan had something to do with Tanya's disappearance?"

"I think it's possible that he had some part in it, yes."

"And then what? Someone found out and killed him, as revenge?"

"Maybe."

"O-kay. And why would they do that? Who would do that? Not Tanya's parents. They're both pushing for answers. If they found out that Tristan killed Tanya, I can't see them killing him and then hounding the police to keep investigating. They'd want his death covered up, not exposed."

"Agreed. I doubt they have anything to do with Tristan's death. And I'm not saying with any degree of confidence that Tristan killed Tanya. I'm just considering that he might have known something about it or have been involved in some way. You heard Peyton talk about having friends in high school. But when I questioned her about them, she said they'd all gone their separate ways, lost touch. You don't get to be a prom queen without being an outgoing, people person, someone who's popular and makes friends wherever they go. She'd have to have had a personality transplant after high school to immediately give all of that up. If she truly hasn't kept tabs on her high-school friends, there has to be a compelling reason. And I'm betting that compelling reason is whatever made her nervous whenever I brought up Tanya."

"I'm following but not following."

She took another swig of beer. "I'm all over the place. I know. This isn't my normal way of investigating, being in a rush, trying to jump from point *A* to point *G* without covering the letters in between. I'm babbling and going off on all kinds of tangents."

"How about we sit, take a deep breath, then talk it through."

"Good idea." She reached for the beer again.

He took it from her and set it in the sink. "Let's keep that brilliant mind of yours operating on all cylinders since we have a limited amount of time. Okay?"

She rolled her eyes but headed to the table, where they sat across from each other.

"Go ahead," he said. "Slowly, for those of us not used to doing investigations like this. What are we looking at so far?"

"So far." She crossed her arms on the tabletop. "All right. Let's talk it through. We have a sophomore, a fifteen-year-old about to become a junior. She's smart, a bookworm, creative, introverted. The reports we read say she didn't have any close friends. Her parents and her books were her only real support system."

"Aside from your sister, right? Cassidy was her teacher and concerned about her."

"Cassidy said that Tanya was very private, hard to get close to. She worried about her not having friends so she'd spoken to her parents several times, becoming close to them. Cassidy is one of those teachers who is usually the favorite, the teacher all the kids adore. But in Tanya's case, she, well, wasn't. I think that's why Tanya's disappearance hit her so hard. She'd tried to be her friend, to be there for her, but never quite managed to break through Tanya's wall."

She gave him a sad smile. "We're back to a young girl pretty much on her own. She goes missing a few weeks after graduation. And after that, one of the most popular seniors, Peyton, cuts off contact with all her friends. Not only that, her main friends from school were at the lake today and ignored not only her, but each other. So it's likely that her friends did the same thing, dropped all of their close acquaintances after graduation. There aren't any huge, traumatic events in town that I've heard of from Cassidy that happened around that time. The only traumatic event was Tanya's disappearance and the fallout from that."

"The police grilling Peyton and her friends, among others."

"Exactly," she said. "And now one of those former friends has died. Not just that, he was murdered. Peyton spoke about him like she still cared for him, and yet she hadn't talked to him in almost a year. Add to that her nervousness, fear really, every time I mentioned Tanya and, well, you can see where I'm going."

"It's all connected."

"Seems like it," she said.

"What if those conclusions we're jumping to are completely wrong?"

"What if they aren't?"

He smiled. "Okay. So other than me performing searches on the lake, once I'm allowed back in that area, you and I are going to spend the rest of our time looking into a group of teenagers to see, what, if one or all of them are killers?"

"Now, that would be jumping to conclusions."

"Normally I consider myself an intelligent man. But keeping up with the twists and turns of your thought process is blowing my confidence."

She laughed. "I'll take that as a compliment. I'm just thinking out loud here. No hard facts, just a lot of assumptions and potential connections, far more questions than answers. All I'm really concluding is that we need to look for a connection between Tristan and Tanya. And follow up on Peyton to see what connections she might have had with either of them. I'm not saying that she or her other friends are killers. Honestly, it doesn't sound plausible since nothing in any of their backgrounds—at least according to the police reports we read—raised any red flags. None of them have police records or have done anything outrageous."

"That we know of."

"Agreed." She shrugged. "But my experience, or instinct, or whatever you want to call it, tells me we've found a thread to follow that might lead us where we want to go.

We should focus on Peyton, Tristan and Tanya, and look for where their paths crossed in the days leading up to Tanya's disappearance, and Tristan's death—once the medical examiner can give us a date range on that."

"Is there another angle we should pursue, in case that one is a dead end?"

"I didn't find anything in the files we read last night that leads me to any other avenues to explore. If I had another month to research and interview people, I'm certain I could come up with something more promising. But time being what it is, this is the best we've got."

"You're the expert. I'll follow your lead. Until Chief Dawson gives me the green light to continue my grid search, I'm free to be the Watson to your Sherlock. What's our next step?"

She grabbed her purse from one of the end tables. "We're heading into town. I'll drive. I'm tired of climbing up in that behemoth truck of yours."

"I don't mind being chauffeured. What's the plan once we get to town?"

"Lunch and eavesdropping."

When they reached her silver Lexus, he held the driver's door open. She smiled her thanks but hesitated, her smile fading as she looked over the car's roof toward the woods behind the cabin.

Kaden turned and scanned the trees as well, but didn't see any cause for alarm. "What is it? Did you hear something?"

Her gaze was still on the woods. "I didn't hear anything. It's just… For a moment, I thought I… The breeze, it smelled like…cologne."

He glanced toward the woods again, studying the shadows. But it was no use. In spite of the bright sunlight today, the gloom of the forest was nearly impenetrable. "Get in the cabin. I'll check it out."

She grabbed his hand. "No. You're not going into the woods alone just because all those flowers my sister has in her yard reminded me of someone. She could practically start her own perfume factory with everything she's planted out here. Come on. Let's go. We have an investigation to run."

When she tried to pull her hand back, he tightened his hold. "Is it Troy? Is that what you're worried about? You think he might have figured out where you are?"

She blinked in surprise. "You remembered his name?"

"Troy Warren. I remember." He glanced at the woods again. "Get in your car. Lock the door. When we get to town, the first thing we're doing is stopping at the police station."

Chapter Eleven

With Troy Warren's picture given to the police, and after Chief Dawson assured them he'd send some deputies to search the area around the cabin for signs of an intruder, Kaden was more at ease. But he was still on high alert just in case Shanna's ex was here in Mystic Lake. Kaden had no intention of letting her out of his sight now, even if that meant sleeping on the couch for the rest of his time here.

As Shanna turned her car into a parking lot behind a large two-story building, Kaden couldn't help but laugh.

"Stella's Bed and Breakfast. Guess you changed your mind about me sharing the cabin, even during the daylight hours."

"I wouldn't dream of kicking out my new assistant, Dr. Watson. My sister's notes about places to go around town included the restaurant attached to the B and B. Aside from a few sandwich shops or the restaurant at the marina, it's pretty much the only place to eat around here. It's supposed to be really good, though."

"Seems unusual to attach a restaurant to a B and B." Kaden got out of the car and headed toward the building with Shanna.

"True, but my sister said the restaurant is the real money

maker for Stella and her husband, Frank. The rooms don't fill up much except during the summer."

"Sounds like Stella is a good businesswoman to have diversified."

"Thanks for noticing," an older woman said as she opened the door for them. "Now, if you'll share that observation with my husband, I might comp a dessert for you. Table for two? You must be Cassidy's sister. Shanna, right? And this handsome man must be your plus-one."

Before Kaden could set her straight, Shanna said, "Yes, ma'am. I keep him along as eye candy."

Kaden choked, then coughed and cleared his throat.

"Does the eye candy have a name?" Stella stepped in after Shanna while Kaden held the door for them.

"He can hear you, you know." Kaden followed them toward a table.

Stella turned around, grinning. "Well, that's one advantage you have over my Frank. He can't hear a thing without his earpiece. You got a name or should I use the one Ms. Shanna called you?"

He held out his hand. "Kaden Rafferty, ma'am."

She pushed his arm away. "Save the handshakes for the men. We're all about Southern warmth here. Give this old woman a hug, young man." Without waiting, she wrapped her arms around his waist.

He froze in surprise, then narrowed his eyes in warning at Shanna, who was obviously struggling not to burst out laughing. He put his arms around Stella and lightly returned the hug.

She pulled back and patted his chest. "He's handsome and strong, Ms. Shanna. And too polite to refuse to hug an elder, even though she's invading his space and making him uncomfortable."

Kaden cleared his throat again. "You're not making me uncomfortable."

Stella rolled her eyes. "I'm sure you're more comfortable hugging pretty Ms. Shanna. You're sweet to indulge me. But we have to get back to business now, before she gets jealous. I'll bring you both some of my famous blueberry muffins hot out of the oven. We serve them all day. Have a seat right over here, in the middle of the room, and take a gander at the menus. This here will give you the best location for listening in on everyone's conversations."

Shanna's eyes widened. "Excuse me?"

Stella waved her into her seat. "Now, don't you be getting upset. I mean no harm. But you're an investigator, right? Cassidy told me about you enough times for it to click. You're looking into that awful business with that young man who drowned at the lake, aren't you? Can't say it's the first drowning around here and it won't be the last. But it's always sad. Anyway, you do what you need to do. Listen in, see what you can figure out about whether he was with someone or not whenever he drowned. I hate to say it but not everyone is a Good Samaritan and will risk themselves to save someone else. If he was with a friend and they refused to help or at least call for help, they deserve punishment fitting that. I'll send Daphne over in a few minutes to take your order."

Kaden sat across from Shanna, shaking his head. "Wow. That was…wow."

"She's a whirlwind, for sure." She arched a brow. "And quite friendly with my plus-one."

He grinned and looked around. "Guess we got lucky getting a table. There aren't many left."

"I figured it would be extra busy after this morning's police activities. Everyone's gathering to talk theories and gossip." She pulled two pocket-size notebooks out of her purse and slid one, along with a pen, across the table. "I came prepared."

"I'm not surprised." He picked up the pen and little pad of paper. "Let the eavesdropping begin."

They both had cheeseburgers, although Shanna ordered hers without bread and he added bacon. But the clock was ticking and they were both mainly focused on gathering information.

As Shanna had predicted, the town gossips were having a field day about the discovery of remains in the lake, and the even more shocking revelation that the person who'd died was one of the town's own. From what Kaden had heard from a group of men sitting behind him, the Cargill family wasn't exactly beloved here in Mystic Lake. They had one of the largest mansions on one of the tallest mountains and, whether true or not, at least gave the impression to many of the townspeople that they thought themselves above them socially, not just literally.

Tristan only associated with the most popular kids, allegedly using his family's wealth as a carrot to buy his way into the school's inner circle despite being somewhat of a nerd. It became clear that the town had given a collective sigh of relief when Tristan headed to Europe for his so-called gap year. No one, it seemed, had any idea that he'd ever returned.

Except for whoever had killed him.

The police had done well to keep the fact that Tristan

had been murdered a secret. So far, at least. The people at the tables near Kaden all seemed to believe it was yet another mysterious accident that could be attributed either to the ghosts of the original people killed when the town was formed, or someone called the Phantom. He underlined *the Phantom* several times, determined to follow up and try to figure out what that was all about.

Across from him, Shanna had her own list going, but hers mostly consisted of names with little comments beside each one. She'd listed Tristan and Tanya in the middle of the page and had drawn lines to each name she added, forming what appeared to be a tree of spaghetti with lines crossing over each other as she apparently linked each name to other names in her tree.

A few minutes after Daphne had taken away their plates, Stella seemed to appear from out of nowhere, leaning over Shanna's shoulder.

"You forgot Jack," she said.

Shanna started, then looked up. "Sorry, what?"

Stella patted her shoulder. "Didn't mean to startle you, honey. Just looking at your little tree there and I noticed you're missing Jack Neal." She tapped an empty spot on the page. "There. Put his name there. He's the local bully around here." She frowned. "Well, one of them. He's sitting over at that table in the far corner with Sam Morton, the former high-school quarterback."

Shanna and Kaden both looked toward the table that Stella had indicated. The plates of food in front of the two young men didn't appear to have been touched. Instead, they were in deep conversation, ignoring everyone around them.

"Wonder what they're talking about," Shanna said. "Seems serious."

Stella shook her head, a look of disgust on her face. “Knowing those two, nothing good. At least, in the old days they’d be up to some foolery. I haven’t seen them together in a long time. Either they’re discussing plans for a party or whose car to egg next. Then again, they haven’t caused much trouble since graduation, so maybe they’ve reformed.”

The look on her face showed her doubt in her own statement. She obviously wasn’t a fan of either of them. She tapped Shanna’s paper. “Jack Neal. Add him to your list. I see you already had Sam on there.”

“Right.” She added the name and drew a line from Jack to Sam.

“Now, draw a line from both of them to Tristan. You’re looking for connections, friends, right? Or at least who they associated with on a regular basis?”

“Yes. Exactly.” Shanna drew the additional lines. “Am I missing anyone else?”

Stella considered a moment, then shook her head. “You’ve got all the names of the popular crowd and a pretty good representation of who was besties with whom.”

Shanna shook her head, a smile curving her lips. “Maybe I should have saved Kaden and me some trouble and just sat down with you today. It would have been faster.”

“Maybe. The memory isn’t what it used to be. I wouldn’t have thought of Jessica DeWalt, former cheerleader, and you’ve got her. Never saw her in here as often as the others. Haven’t seen her around in a while. What’s that line you drew from Tristan to Tanya? Far as I know they weren’t friends.”

“The line means there’s something they have in common, that both of them appear to have, ah, drowned in the lake.”

"And you're wondering if there's another connection? Like foul play?"

Shanna motioned for her to keep her voice down. "I don't know that at all. I'm just keeping an open mind until we find Tanya."

Stella put a hand on her hip. "Now, don't you go telling half truths, Ms. Shanna. That'll put you on my bad side quicker than anything."

Her face reddened, like a child caught with their hand in a cookie jar. It was a struggle for Kaden not to laugh. She really was adorable.

"That's not my intention," Shanna said. "I'm just…trying to be quiet about it. I don't want to spout any theories without proof. And, honestly, we really don't have a theory just yet. Other than that it's odd for two kids from the same school to die the same way, allegedly, anyway. We won't know for sure, of course, until we locate Tanya."

Shanna pointed to the page. "I haven't heard of any friends for Tanya. Do you know of any?"

Stella pursed her lips as she studied the page. "Poor little Tanya was pretty much a bookworm. Nice to everyone but never hung out with other kids that I know of. Her parents and her studies were what kept her company. The others on your list, well, they were the popular ones, though I never did understand why. You could put everyone's name from their graduating class on that chart since they all knew the popular kids. If you're looking for close ties, then you've pretty much covered the main clique that hung together. Let's see, the prom queen, the quarterback, the rich kid, the cheerleader and, of course, Jack, the resident bully. That's the gang. But I don't think Tanya should be on that page at all. She was a sophomore. The rest were seniors.

They wouldn't have hung out with her. Whatever happened to that child has nothing to do with Tristan or the kids he hung with. Then again, I'm not the investigator. So what do I know?" She shrugged and stepped back, as if to leave.

"Stella," Kaden said, stopping her. "I don't suppose you can help me with a name." He turned his pad of paper toward her and pointed.

Her eyebrows raised. "The Phantom? What's a myth for tourists have to do with what you're investigating?"

"Humor me?"

She glanced around the room. "Guess everything's under control for now. I'll give you a few more minutes."

Kaden rushed to pull a chair back for her. She raised her eyebrows and sat.

"Your mama taught you manners, young man. Reminds me of another big, strapping fellow around here. Handsome, like you. Now, who am I thinking of?" She frowned and tapped her fingers on the tabletop. "Aw, yes. Aidan O'Brien. Even now, he's more of a recluse, doesn't come around much or have much use for most of the people here in town. But he always treats me like a queen." She patted Kaden's shoulder, as if he'd somehow passed a personal test of hers.

"He's Officer Grace O'Brien's husband, right?" Shanna asked.

"He sure is. Father of little Alannah. Such a sweet child. Pretty, too. When she grows up she's going to have her daddy sweating when all the boys start coming around." She chuckled. "But that's not why you're here. What was it you asked about? Ah, yes. That silly Phantom story."

Kaden smiled, not buying her claim that she'd forgotten anything, even for a minute. This woman might be approaching seventy, but her mind was every bit as sharp as someone decades younger.

She crossed her arms and sat back in her chair. "You might do better asking one of the natives for more information. I'm a transplant, only been here a few years past a decade. Even this B and B has been here far longer than me, built before I ever knew Mystic Lake existed." She smiled. "But I can tell you what I've heard. Mainly it's the kids who spread the rumors. I've never seen one piece of evidence that this Phantom exists. I swear every year the next class of kids at school adds more to the myth, embellishing and pretending they've seen this Phantom out in the woods by the lake or hiding up in the mountains. They'll tell you he's half-man, half-fish, that he has gills and can swim underwater. Every time someone falls off a boat around here and never resurfaces, they blame it on this Phantom, say he's the one who pulled them overboard and held their bodies under water."

She shrugged. "Others swear he lives in the caves in the mountains, that he uses old forgotten mines around town to move around without being detected. Some kids have said he's got a beard to his belly and is covered with fur, like Sasquatch. All I know for a fact is that sometimes people's food, clothing and other supplies disappear from their vacation homes or hunting cabins up in the mountains. Heck, I've even had stuff go missing here, but I've always figured it was the local kids, not some ghost. Beau, Police Chief Dawson, does his best to look into those reports. When he does catch someone, it always ends up being exactly what you'd expect. Kids up to no good."

Kaden rested his forearms on the table. "So you don't think the Phantom actually exists? He's not someone we should be looking at who might have something to do with the death of Tristan? Or Tanya's disappearance?"

She waved her hand in the air as if waving away the theory. "You'd be wasting your time in my opinion. I think this whole Phantom thing was made up as a way for kids to scare each other, like telling ghost stories around a campfire. Or, even more likely, a way for unscrupulous adults to build up yet another story about Mystic Lake to make it seem mysterious. Tourists love things like that. And tourists mean money for the town. Hard to blame anyone when you put it in that perspective. A harmless made-up myth to help them put food on the table."

She shoved back her chair and stood. "That's about all the time I can spare right now. Frank will be yelling for me to come help with the dishes soon. And I need to keep after the waiters and waitresses to keep the fear of Stella in 'em." She winked and hurried toward the doorway that led into the kitchen.

Kaden sat back. "I can't see Dawson using his limited resources to chase a legend and search what's likely to be hundreds of caves up in the mountains. And sending his people into old abandoned mine shafts would be far too dangerous."

"Aimlessly searching through the woods for Tanya wouldn't be the best use of our time, either. As much as I loathe the idea of causing the Jerichos any more pain, I feel we should talk to them. Maybe they can shed some light on whether there could potentially be any link from Tanya to Tristan or the other popular kids."

Kaden cocked his head, considering. "If Tanya had no friends because she was shy, socially awkward, but was desperate for company, what might she do?"

Shanna shrugged. "Crash a party? That's the best way to meet a lot of other kids in one location outside of school. But that doesn't really work in this case since she disappeared a few weeks after school was over, after graduation."

"When do people plan all those post-graduation parties? While school is still in session. She could have overheard someone in the hallway talking about parties happening in the weeks after school was out and decided to show up at one uninvited. But someone didn't like that she was there."

"And they killed her because of it? That seems weak."

"Because you're assuming they did it on purpose. Maybe it was an accident. The police theory was that she went to that picnic area we were at this morning and ended up going down to the lake, maybe fell in and drowned. What if there was a party out there and she was pushed in, instead of falling in? The area is remote enough that it's unlikely anyone would have seen it happen."

She slowly shook her head. "Where did you come up with that idea? There's nothing to base it on."

"It's based on the belief that she was in that area, the picnic grounds, before she disappeared, which is based on interviews with her parents. Add to that we both know it could be the perfect party spot for a bunch of high schoolers. They could even light a bonfire out there without getting much attention. Think about it. Tristan was found in the lake right there. And we feel that Tanya could be there, too. If she never associated with this so-called clique, but one of them and her are found in the same area, an end-of-the-year bash and her crashing it fits."

"Okay, yes, it could fit. But it's still completely speculation."

"True, but there is one other thing that makes it sound

plausible, or at least something to further explore. Stella told us the group that formed the most popular clique at that school quit seeing each other for the most part after graduation. Peyton told you that graduation night was the last time she's pretty much seen the others. If something bad happened out by the lake, it makes sense why they'd all take a vow of silence, or whatever, then stay away from each other in the hopes that none of them would talk."

She shot a look at the corner table. "Maybe we should ask Sam and Jack about any end-of-the-year parties, or at least, whether they frequented that area where Tristan's remains were found. I'd rather get more information from them before I bother the Jerichos."

They both stood and gathered their notes.

French doors off the side of the restaurant burst open and an older man hobbled inside, eyes wide, face pale. "Somebody help! There's a woman lying in the ditch. I can't pull her out." He headed back outside, leaving the doors open behind him.

Shanna exchanged a startled glance with Kaden. Then they were both running outside as she used her cell phone to dial 911. It seemed as if the entire restaurant was emptying behind them as they raced across the grassy side yard toward where the much slower white-haired man was pointing.

Kaden was the first to reach the ditch and saw the nude body of a young woman half in and half out of the water. Her fingers clutched the green grass as if she was trying to pull herself up onto the bank. But the rest of her, from her hips down, was still beneath the water. Her eyes were closed.

He slid down the incline and pressed his fingers against

the side of her neck, which he noted had two burn marks. A Taser? Stun gun? He couldn't find a pulse, and she was cold. He quickly pulled her out of the water. Then he put her on his shoulder and climbed up to the level grassy area.

After gently laying her down, he swiped her long dark hair back from her face.

"No-o-o-o!" The scream resonated through the crowd.

He jerked his head up to see Peyton Holloway framed in the French doors of the restaurant, her mouth now covered with her hands.

Shanna dropped down beside Kaden as he began chest compressions on the young woman.

"Police are on the way," she said. "They don't have an ambulance or hospital around here. They're sending a medevac chopper from the local marina. Apparently, the owner doubles as a chopper pilot and Stella rides with him to take patients to the hospital in Chattanooga. I asked one of the patrons to get Stella. I'm surprised she's not here already with all the commotion going on."

He nodded, silently keeping count of compressions. Once he hit thirty, he pinched the woman's nose closed and blew a quick deep breath into her mouth, watching to ensure that her chest rose. After a second breath, he felt her carotid again. Still no pulse. He started compressions again.

"Out of the way, people. Move." Stella suddenly burst through the crowd, her knees popping as Shanna helped her down across from Kaden. She was carrying a red box with the picture of a heart on it and a jagged electrical line going down the middle—an automated external defibrillator.

Stella glanced at the woman's face, then gasped. "It's Jessica DeWalt." She shook her head in sympathy as she quickly affixed two patches on the woman's chest, one below and one to the side of where Kaden was doing compressions.

"Okay," she said. "Kaden, stop. Shanna, back up. Make sure neither of you are touching her."

Kaden grabbed Shanna around her waist and scooted her back several feet.

She smiled her thanks, tears in her eyes as she looked at DeWalt, the young cheerleader with her entire future ahead of her.

A light on the AED went green. Stella pressed it, sending electricity sizzling through the leads to the pads on DeWalt's chest. Her body jumped, but her eyes remained closed. Her chest was still, no breaths filling her lungs.

Stella pressed a stethoscope against the woman's chest. "She's cold."

"Hypothermia?" Kaden asked.

Her haunted gaze met his. "Even in the mountains this time of year, I don't think it's cold enough for that. I think we're too late."

Kaden immediately began compressions again. "Recharge, Stella."

"It's charging. Just a couple more seconds." The light turned green. "Everyone clear."

Kaden sat back and watched Stella deliver another shock. She listened with her stethoscope again and shook her head.

"Charge it." He continued compressions. How old was this woman? Eighteen? Nineteen? Too young to die. Stella was wrong, had to be. The cold mountain water running through the ditch must have cooled her body, putting her into shock. How many times had he heard about someone being submerged in an icy cold lake and later being revived? The cold water had slowed down their brain activity, allowed them to survive.

Twenty-eight. Twenty-nine. Thirty. He stopped and blew two deep breaths.

"Clear," Stella said, the urgency gone from her voice.

He pulled back, waited for the zip of electricity to flow into the woman's body.

Kaden watched as Stella listened through her stethoscope, then shook her head.

"Damn it. Again, Stella. Again." He began compressions as the machine charged.

"Kaden." Shanna's hand touched his shoulder. "She's gone. Jessica's gone."

He shook off her hand. "Stella? Is it ready?"

"Ready," Stella said. "Clear."

He leaned back, holding his arms out to make sure that Shanna was safely out of danger as well.

A blast of air was accompanied by a loud *thwap-thwap-thwap* sound. Kaden and Shanna looked up to see the medevac chopper hovering out on the street in front of the B and B as it slowly lowered.

The sound of a ragged cough had Kaden jerking his head back around.

"My God," Stella whispered. "She's breathing." She stared at him in shock.

Kaden looked down, his own breath catching as he looked into a pair of light brown eyes. "It's okay," he whispered brokenly. "You're safe, Jessica."

Her eyes welled up with tears.

"A blanket," Stella ordered. "We need to warm her and—"

Kaden was already pulling his shirt over his head. He

placed it over the small woman, covering her from chest to thigh.

"Back up, folks. Back up." The man from the chopper rushed over with a rolling gurney.

Kaden started to rise, but the girl grabbed his hand, clinging to it. "D-don't let h-h-him get m-me. D-d-don't—"

"Shh," Shanna whispered, crossing to Kaden's other side and gently feathering the girl's hair back from her cheeks. "You're safe. No one is going to hurt you again. The chopper pilot—"

"Mr. Thompson," the man said, his voice calm and soothing. "Jessica, it's Bobby. We're taking you to the hospital, okay?"

She frowned. "Billy Bob?"

He grinned. "Stop with the Billy and Billy Bob stuff. I prefer Bobby and you know it."

A tear slid down her cheek.

Thompson grimaced. "I'm teasing. Call me whatever you want, sweetie. We're going to take care of you. Let, Mr. ah—"

"Rafferty. Call me Kaden."

Bobby nodded. "You need to let Kaden's hand go, Jessica, so we can take you on a chopper ride."

She nodded, still crying, but finally let go of Kaden's hand.

"Stella, where's she hurt?" Bobby asked, motioning toward the gurney. "Do we need the backboard and neck brace?"

Kaden's breath caught. He'd been so intent on getting her out of the water and reviving her that he hadn't considered the possibility of broken bones. *God, please don't let her be paralyzed.*

“Grab the brace and backboard as a precaution.” Stella leaned over, meeting the girl’s tortured gaze. “Jessica, are you hurting anywhere? Any broken bones?”

“N-neck. Burns.”

Stella checked Jessica’s neck. Then her gaze shot to Kaden.

He nodded, silently mouthing the words *stun gun*.

“Ch-chest hurts,” Jessica whispered. “On…fire.”

Guilt slammed through Kaden. Had he been too rough with his compressions? Broken some ribs?

Stella, as if sensing his turmoil, gave him a reassuring look. “We’ll take care of that. Bobby’s going to put a brace on your neck to make you comfortable.” She moved to give Bobby room, holding the girl’s head still as he put the neck brace on her. As he positioned the backboard beside her, Stella asked, “Do you hurt anywhere else?”

“All… All over. Sore. C-cold.” Her voice was strained, her brow furrowed in obvious pain.

“We’re going to roll you on your side really carefully and put a hard board under you to protect your back, okay? I’ll hold your head while Kaden and Bobby roll you and slide the board under.”

“O-okay. Th-thank you.” Her voice seemed to be getting weaker.

Stella gave Bobby a sharp look and whispered, “Hurry. I’ll get her vitals in the chopper.”

Kaden helped with Bobby’s directions. Soon, Jessica was on the backboard and they were strapping her onto the gurney.

Kaden pushed the gurney while Bobby guided it and helped rush Jessica to the chopper. In a matter of seconds, she was loaded, along with Stella, and the chopper began its ascent.

The sound of sirens filled the air as a police car raced

up the road on this side of the lake, coming from the direction of the marina toward the B and B.

"The cavalry is finally here," Shanna said. "I'd hate being them right now, with so much happening. They have to be stretched pretty thin."

Kaden nodded, looking at the crowd gathered outside the restaurant. "Where did Peyton go?"

Shanna slid an arm around his waist, startling him. He looked down in question.

"I don't care about Peyton right now." She pressed a hand against his chest, her soft warm fingers against his bare skin heating him like fire. "How are you? That was an awful, traumatic thing to go through. Are you okay?"

He slowly shook his head in wonder. "You're worried about me? You went through it, too."

"It's not the same. You had her life in your hands. And even though Stella and I were ready to let go, you didn't. You saved her, Kaden. You saved a life." She stepped closer, pressing her cheek against his chest as she hugged him.

In spite of his vow to keep things cool between the two of them, he was powerless to stop himself as he tightened his arms around her and rested his cheek on the top of her head. The feel of her in his arms, her warmth cradled against his naked chest, made the agony of almost being unable to save a dying girl begin to fade. As Shanna had reminded him, the woman hadn't died. They'd given her a chance at a future. And that was the best feeling of all.

"Get a room," a man's voice said close to them, laughter heavy in his tone.

Shanna stiffened, then quickly pulled away, her cheeks flushing a light pink.

Kaden frowned at an amused-looking Chief Dawson. "You're late. And your timing sucks."

Dawson's smile faded as he glanced around at the chattering onlookers. "Yeah. I know. When the call came in about another body being found, Officers Fletcher and Collier were searching around Mrs. Tate's cabin for signs of the Warren guy. Ortiz and O'Brien were responding to a medical emergency and I was at the lake with the Chattanooga diving team. Days like this, I sure wish I had more than four deputies. I saw the chopper head out. I'm hoping that's a good sign? I don't need to call the medical examiner? Again?"

"Jessica DeWalt is alive," Kaden said. "Or, she was, when we loaded her onto the chopper."

"DeWalt." Dawson shook his head, clearly surprised to hear that name.

"Kaden saved her," Shanna said.

"With help," he corrected. "It was a team effort. There wasn't any blood or obvious injuries that I saw. But there were two parallel burn marks on her neck."

"Stun gun?"

"I think so, yes."

Dawson swore. "What else?"

"When I found her, she was naked, lying in the ditch, unresponsive. We had to revive her. Thank God that Stella was here with a defibrillator."

Dawson raked his hands through his short hair. "What's going on around here? DeWalt's a kid. Why would anyone want to hurt her?" He let out a deep breath, then motioned toward Kaden's chest. "We're about the same size. I'll grab you a shirt from the go bag in my patrol car."

Chapter Twelve

Shanna threaded her way through the still-crowded restaurant while Kaden finished briefing Dawson on the other side of the room. The chief had asked everyone to stay, so his recently arrived deputies, Christopher Collier and Liza Fletcher, could interview them as potential witnesses. But Shanna couldn't seem to locate the people *she* wanted to speak to.

"Hey, everything okay?" Kaden stopped beside her.

"I guess so, except that I can't find Peyton, Sam, or Jack. Do you know whether they were already interviewed?"

He motioned toward Collier and Fletcher, sitting at a table near the French doors. "They've only spoken to a few people so far. I don't remember seeing the ones you mentioned over there yet. But I was speaking to Dawson, so I could have missed them. I wanted to give you an update about the search by your cabin. Nothing was found. No indications that anyone had been in those woods anytime recently."

"That's a relief. I guess. Honestly, I'd rather know for sure where Troy is these days rather than him being in the wind. But as long as he's not here in Mystic Lake, that's good."

"I'd feel better if you stick close to me for now on. It's

not just Troy that we need to be on guard against, it's whoever is terrorizing this town."

"No need to convince me. I'm happy to have a tall, buff man as my bodyguard."

He grinned. "And I'm happy to keep an eye on you."

She smiled and motioned toward the chief, who was talking to one of the potential witnesses. "Has Dawson gotten any updates about Jessica?"

"Not yet. He already notified the family. They live close by and are on their way to the hospital right now. He'll text me once he hears anything on her condition."

"Good. Are we free to leave?" she asked. "He doesn't need to question us further?"

"We can go. You have somewhere specific in mind?"

"Talking to the remaining members of the popular clique is near the top of my list. But I'd like to see the Jerichos first. They deserve to be updated about what happened here in case the rumors start up about connections to Tristan, and then potentially to Tanya. I don't want them caught off guard like when they were told by the police that we were here working their daughter's case."

"You have their address?"

"I'm hoping they haven't moved since last spring, when Tanya went missing. I programmed their address from the police files into my phone for when it came time to go see them. It's time."

RAYMOND AND LYDIA JERICHO were nothing like Shanna had expected, or at least that's what she thought when she and Kaden had first arrived at their home. From Cassidy's comments about how devastated they were, Shanna had assumed they'd be broken, barely able to function. They were definitely somber. But they were also polite and welcoming.

In spite of Shanna and Kaden's insistences that they didn't need anything, Lydia had brought them ice-cold glasses of sweet tea and placed crystal bowls of pretzels and nuts on the coffee table in front of them, along with little cocktail napkins. It wasn't until Kaden began explaining what had happened at the B and B that the cracks in their facades began to show. Shanna realized they were putting on a brave face for the world. But the truth revealed itself in how Raymond's hands shook as he sat quietly listening. And in the streaks of white that peppered Lydia's dark hair that shouldn't have begun to gray for many more years. Inside, their battered souls were being held together with tattered threads of hope that wouldn't sustain them much longer. They were a dam ready to break. And she desperately didn't want to be the one to burst that dam wide open and destroy them.

Shanna stood. Kaden gave her a surprised glance then stood as well.

"You're leaving already?" Lydia rose and took Shanna's hands in hers. "I thought you wanted to discuss Tanya, that you had questions."

Shanna lightly squeezed the woman's cold, thin fingers. "I did. We do. But now isn't the right time. We can come back later and—"

Lydia's hold changed, gripping hers with surprising strength in spite of how frail she appeared. "Please. Don't leave. Not yet. Ask us any questions you have. We want to help. We want your help." Her mouth formed the ghost of a smile that probably hadn't curved her lips in months. "We're stronger than we look, Ms. Hudson. If there's any chance you can find our little girl, no matter what has happened to her, we want her found." She let go and sat beside her husband, who put his arm around her shoulders, and waited.

Kaden gently took Shanna's hand, and lightly tugged her down beside him as they sat once again. Feeling as if she needed as much support as poor Mr. and Mrs. Jericho, right now, Shanna subtly moved closer to Kaden, taking comfort in his strength and warmth.

"Go ahead." This time, it was Mr. Jericho who spoke. "Please."

For the next half hour, Shanna carefully led the grieving parents down the path she wanted to take. But she did it by having them tell her about Tanya, her likes and dislikes, what she preferred to do with her free time. While Shanna mentally logged the details that would help her understand a typical day for the missing girl, and the people she associated with on a regular basis, Kaden sat quietly beside her. He seemed content to trust her as an investigator and only spoke up a few times to clarify his own understanding of some details that had been shared.

While Shanna was getting a good picture of Tanya and how she liked to spend her time, her parents hadn't said anything about the popular crowd, like Peyton and the others. The few classmates the Jerichos mentioned were other smart kids in the academic top ten. Tanya had plenty in common with them. But there'd been nothing said about them going anywhere together. No trips into Chattanooga for a girl's day of shopping, or to see a movie. No trips to a concert or a ball game. No stories about any of them ever visiting her at her home, or vice versa. Was it because Tanya didn't want any friends? Or was it because the friends she had, she didn't speak about to her parents.

The Jerichos seemed like nice people who loved their daughter more than anything. But that kind of love, while well-intentioned, could also feel smothering to a girl on the cusp of becoming a woman. Did Tanya have a crush on some boy and was afraid to tell them because they'd be worried about the impact on her grades, potentially ruining her chance to go to college on a full scholarship? Or was it something insidious, like bullying? Shanna had been that smart, studious girl at school, too. She knew how awful other kids could be, singling her out for being different, for not fitting in. Would Tanya tell her parents about things like that? Or would she keep that a secret, be too embarrassed to tell them. Or too scared that if she did, they'd try to help her by going to her teachers about it, making her even more of a target for bullies?

Somehow, Shanna had to find out what secrets Tanya kept from her parents, assuming there were any. And the only person who could tell her that was Tanya.

When there was a break in the conversation, Shanna smiled. "Mrs. Jericho—"

"Lydia. Please."

"Lydia. Would you mind if we—Kaden and I—sit in Tanya's bedroom for a few minutes? Alone? It would help us get more of a feel for her true personality by experiencing the feeling of her room, how she decorated it, what she looked at every day. Would that be okay?"

The woman frowned and glanced at her husband. He gave Shanna a knowing look, as if he understood her true goal. And supported it. Perhaps he knew more about Tanya than her mother and was unwilling to say it in front of her. He squeezed her shoulder and smiled. "It's okay, Lydia. They're trying to find our little girl."

She chewed her lip, obviously struggling with the idea of them being in Tanya's room.

Raymond nodded at Shanna and Kaden. "It's the last room on the left, down that hallway behind you. Take as long as you need."

Lydia frowned. "Ray—"

"It's okay. Here, I'll help you clear away the food and drinks."

Shanna nodded her thanks as she and Kaden hurried out of the room.

Once inside Tanya's bedroom, Kaden quietly closed the door behind them and raised an eyebrow. "Looks like a princess theme park threw up in here. I've never seen so much pink and purple in one room. What are we searching for, Sherlock?"

"Secrets, dear Watson."

"Like a diary?"

"Exactly like a diary."

"On it." Kaden flipped the pink comforter up on top of the mattress.

"Careful," Shanna whispered. "We need to leave the room exactly like we found it. I don't want to upset Lydia."

"I'll put it back once I search under the mattress."

"It won't be under the mattress, assuming she has one. That's too easy." She headed for the tall bookshelf on the other side of the room, its shelves sagging beneath the weight of all the books stacked on them. "It will be somewhere else, like maybe—"

"Here?"

She turned around to see him pulling out a small book from beneath the mattress. It was purple with gold-edged pages and a gold lock on the front holding it closed. "No way."

He thumped the cover with big gold letters that spelled out *Diary*. "Way."

"Gimme, gimme."

He grinned as he handed it to her and rearranged the comforter to look as if they hadn't touched it.

Shanna tugged at the lock. "It's cheap and will break easily. But I don't want to do that to something that might end up being a keepsake. We need a key, or something similar that I can use to—"

"Jimmy the lock?" Kaden held up a pocketknife and flipped open one of the smaller blades.

Shanna shook her head. "I'm not feeling needed here at all."

"What kind of Watson would I be if I wasn't helpful? Want me to open it?"

She crossed her arms. "Go ahead. Don't scratch or break it."

He inserted the knife tip into the tiny lock and turned. The cheap closure snapped open just as if he'd used a key.

"That was a little too easy for you." She took the now open diary from him. "Perhaps I should run a background check to see if you've been cat burgling on the side. I'll take a quick look through this. Can you check out the bookshelf? Maybe she hid pictures or books behind the ones in front that can tell us things she's been doing that she might not have told her parents."

"You picked up on that, too, huh. They seem well-intentioned. But I imagine a fifteen- or sixteen-year-old girl might feel smothered by all that close attention."

She stared at him, surprised to hear his words echoing her earlier thoughts. "Having been that young girl in a similar situation, I absolutely agree."

He tilted some books on the top shelf, looking behind them. "Did you keep a diary, too?"

"Oh, heck no. I wouldn't dare have put my secrets down in writing for someone to find."

"Then what makes you think Tanya did?"

"Honestly, it was a toss-up as to whether we'd find a diary here. I was more interested in looking through the books to see if she wrote her thoughts in some of those or slid pictures and notes in them. But everyone is different. A lot of girls do keep diaries. I just hope hers isn't a cover and has some real information." She continued to turn pages, skimming through it.

"A cover?" He slid the books back and started checking the next shelf.

"Well, if your mom keeps close tabs, you might put a fake diary under your mattress. The real stuff would be..." She looked up as he turned toward her. "Don't you dare tell me you found something."

"I can put it back if you want."

She blew out an exasperated breath and held out her hand.

He gave her two pictures, then bent down to examine the larger books on the bottom shelf.

Shanna's heart seemed to squeeze in her chest as she looked at the photos. They were slightly blurry, as if they'd been taken from far away or in a hurry and Tanya had zoomed in. Both showed the five popular kids that she and Kaden were looking into. The first one was of a bonfire in the woods. The second was at an outdoor pizza joint. There wasn't a sixth seat waiting for Tanya to take it. She obviously wasn't part of the group. Did she long to be one of the popular kids? Part of their inner circle? Or had she taken the picture for another reason? Like maybe she couldn't stand the group and was trying to figure out how to pay them back for some slight, real or imagined.

Shanna snapped her own pictures of Tanya's photos using her phone. After finishing flipping through the diary and concluding that it was indeed likely a made up rosy story of her life for the benefit of her snooping mother—because no one's life was this sanitized and happy—she slid the diary back where Kaden had found it. Then she crossed to the bookshelf.

"Where did you find these?"

He was crouched down, studying the lowest row of books. "Top shelf, middle. Page eighty-three of *The Scarlet Letter*."

"Go, Tanya. I loved that book." She pulled it out and inserted the pictures in the right spot.

"Seriously? You liked it? Wasn't it required reading in high-school English class?"

"Yes, but I still loved it." She narrowed her eyes at him. "Please tell me you read *Wuthering Heights*. And liked it."

"I'll plead the Fifth."

She shook her head. "I don't even know what to say."

"I sense five whacks across the knuckles with a wooden ruler in my future."

"Now where can I find a wooden ruler." She blinked at one of the books on the bottom shelf. "Is that a school yearbook?"

He tilted his head to read the spine. "Looks like. From last year."

They exchanged a sharp look.

Kaden pulled out the book and set it on the bed. Shanna flipped it open, then sighed. "Oh, Tanya. Poor thing."

"What? I don't see anything."

"Exactly. No one signed her yearbook. At least, not the inside cover." She flipped to the end. "They didn't sign the back cover, either. Even casual acquaintances sign each other's yearbooks."

"Maybe her mother didn't want her messing it up by having people write in it." He motioned around the room. "Look how spotless this bedroom is."

"Good point. Where's the senior student section?"

"She was a sophomore. Oh, you want to look for the popular clique."

"Exactly." She thumbed through the pictures, stopping at the section for last names starting with a *C*. "No way."

Kaden leaned over her shoulder. "Four stars below Tristan Cargill's picture. I'm guessing that means she liked him?"

"Did you even go to high school?"

He laughed. "Guess I missed some of the more important parts of my education."

"I'll say. Yes, she liked him. *Really* liked him. Although I don't see how. Sounds like he was a jerk, God rest his soul. Ugh. I shouldn't criticize the dead."

"I don't think he cares at this point."

She lightly punched him on the shoulder. "Who's next in the alphabet?"

"Jessica DeWalt. I'm guessing we skip her since she put the stars on a boy's picture. Sam Morton is the next guy in the clique."

"Morton, Morton." She flipped several more pages, then stopped.

"There," Kaden said. "Bottom right."

"Oh, wow. I wouldn't have recognized him. He sure changed since high school. A lot more clean-cut. A lot less hair."

"And five stars. Looks like we have our connection."

"Looks like. Just for kicks, I'll check out Jack Neal. Want to bet how many stars before I get to his photo?"

"Wasn't he the one Stella said was a bully?"

Shanna turned one more page, then froze. "Oh, my."

Kaden shook his head as he studied the picture. "What the heck did he do to her?"

"Whatever it was, it was bad. I mean, you don't draw devil's horns and knives piercing someone's skull unless you're really upset at them." She took a picture of that as well and then handed the yearbook to Kaden to return it to the shelf.

"I think we've got what we came for," she said, when he joined her by the bed again. "We know there was a connection between Tanya and the others. Or, at least, Tanya wanted there to be a connection. The real question is whether they all knew it and took advantage of her in some way."

"Like hurt her? Or killed her? You really think a group of seniors would murder a sophomore because, what, she was bugging them too much or got caught spying on them?"

"In my line of work, honestly, it wouldn't surprise me. Just like people go nuts with road rage and do things they'd never dream of under normal circumstances. People can be horrible to each other, given the right conditions."

"Or wrong ones," he said.

She nodded her agreement. "Hopefully we can find out the truth about Tanya's last day by aiming targeted questions and putting pressure on Peyton, Sam and Jack."

He got up and held open the bedroom door. "Assuming we can find them."

Chapter Thirteen

Having left Shanna's car parked farther down the mountain in the hopes that Peyton wouldn't notice it, Kaden now stood with Shanna on the road in front of the Holloway home. To call the massive, two-story structure a log cabin seemed like an oxymoron. There was certainly nothing rustic about it. It was elegant, stately and, in spite of its size, it seemed to complement its natural surroundings as if it was always supposed to be here. Situated near the top of one of Mystic Lake's higher mountains, it had nearly 360-degree views from expansive windows on both levels. A wide, wraparound porch gave it a homey feel and easy access to every part of the property.

"Well," Shanna said. "I can see why Peyton hasn't moved out of her parents' house yet. If I lived in something this sweet, I'd never want to leave."

"It's stunning, for sure. But I'd rather struggle not to capsize in hurricane swells than have to tackle that steep, narrow road up the mountain every day. Can you imagine making that drive in ice and snow?"

"Actually, yes. I do live in West Virginia."

"Touché. Your house is at the top of a mountain, too?"

"It would be, if I had the type of money to afford it. But looking up from the foothills isn't exactly a hardship. And

I can drive up the mountains anytime I want for that top-of-the-world feeling. Let me guess, you live right on the water in Charleston?"

"When your bread and butter involves boating, it's the sensible thing to do."

"Tell you what. If you ever visit me in the winter, you can close your eyes while I drive us to the best sightseeing elevations."

"And if you visit me in Charleston, I'll..." He hesitated, remembering her most deep-seated fear. "I promise not to take you anywhere near the water."

She rolled her eyes. "You live on the water. What are you going to do, waste money on a hotel just because of my ridiculous phobia?"

He took her hand in his and pressed a kiss against her knuckles. "It's not ridiculous. Even if you never tell me the cause, or don't even know why you're afraid, the fear is real and nothing to be ashamed of. I would be more than happy to wine and dine you at the most expensive accommodations Charleston has to offer, miles from the coast. You're worth it."

She stared at her hand in his, her eyes suspiciously misty.

He grinned. "Did that sound as sappy to you as it did to me?"

The corner of her mouth twitched. "A little. But it's still the best pickup line anyone's ever tried on me." Her smile faded. "If only you lived in West Virginia."

He squeezed her hand and let go, not voicing what they both were thinking.

If only he didn't live near the one thing that terrified her, the one thing he relied on day in and day out to earn a living.

Hoping to get them back on track, he motioned toward the house. “I don’t see any cars. But I doubt they park on the street or even in the driveway with that four-car garage off to the right.”

“There’s only one way to know for sure.” She jogged across the road and started up the walkway toward the house.

Kaden swore and hurried to catch up. In spite of her earlier speech about being glad her ex wasn’t in Mystic Lake, he’d heard the wobble in her voice. She wasn’t convinced that the police were right, that Troy hadn’t been outside of their cabin. Until Kaden knew for certain, he’d play it safe and assume the creep was in town. Which meant sticking close to Shanna so her ex wouldn’t get a chance to hurt her.

He scanned the bushes along the home’s foundation as they climbed the porch steps. The bushes made great hiding places for someone up to no good. But in an exclusive area like this, odds were that a cowardly stalker ex wouldn’t risk being seen. There were security cameras on every porch, every garage. No one was coming up this mountain road without being caught on several security videos. Hopefully Peyton wasn’t one of the ones keeping an eye on those videos and wouldn’t know they were there.

When Shanna rang the doorbell and the musical chimes played a tune, she burst out laughing. “AC/DC? ‘Highway to Hell’? Do you think the parents know?”

“If they do, they’ve got a great sense of humor.”

“If they don’t, I’ll bet their daughter secretly laughs every time someone comes to visit.”

After a few more rings and several knocks went unanswered, Shanna’s shoulders slumped in disappointment.

"Our plan to try to catch Peyton off guard is a bust. No one's home, not even her parents. Or the maid. Or the butler."

"My, aren't you the snob," Kaden said. "I doubt they have a butler."

She laughed. "Maybe not."

The sound of a car engine coming up the gravel road had both of them turning.

"Blue Mazda," Shanna announced.

"Peyton. If she sees us, she'll probably turn around and take off." He motioned toward the bushes beside the porch steps.

"Oh, heck no." She held up her hands as if to ward him off. "I'm not hiding down there with all the creepy-crawlies."

"Then we'd better run." He grabbed her hand and they took off across the wrap-around porch, not slowing until they rounded the corner at the back right side of the house.

Shanna lightly punched his arm and then bent over, struggling to catch her breath. "How are you not breathing hard?"

"You need to work on your cardio exercise."

"Whatever." She peeked around the corner, then hurriedly ducked back. "She's coming up the driveway."

Moments later, a low hum sounded as one of the garage doors raised.

She looked around the corner again. "The car's parked. There, she's coming out, heading toward the house." She jerked back, both of them being quiet as the sound of shoes crunching on gravel announced Peyton's location.

This time, Kaden leaned around the corner to take a look. "Clear," he whispered. "Go."

As quietly as they could, they raced across the side

porch, rounding the corner to the front as Peyton pushed open the door. She blinked at them, her eyes widening in dismay, before she rushed inside.

Kaden reached the door just as it was about to close. He shoved both hands against it and angled his shoe in the opening to keep her from closing it.

Red spots of anger dotted her cheeks. “Let go of the door. Back off or I’ll call the police.”

Beside Kaden, Shanna held up her phone screen showing the copy of the bonfire picture that he’d found hidden in Tanya’s bookshelf. When Peyton saw it, all the color seemed to drain out of her face.

Peyton’s throat worked. “Where—where did you get that?”

“Kaden found it in one of Tanya Jericho’s books.” She lowered the phone. “Would you like to explain the picture to us or the police? Choose.”

Peyton slowly opened the door.

SHANNA SET HER phone on the coffee table, turning it around so that Peyton could see the damning picture.

Peyton stared at it, twisting her hands together on the couch across from the one where Shanna and Kaden were sitting.

“You lied to us,” Shanna said. “At my sister’s cabin, you swore you’d never even met Tanya, that you and your friends never hung out with her. And yet, here’s a selfie she took with you and your friends in the background, out in the woods having a bonfire. Explain that.”

Peyton’s chin lifted defiantly. “You just explained it yourself. It’s a selfie. She must have been in the woods, snooping on us, and took that. We didn't even know she was there. She's hiding in the bushes. Can't you tell?"

"Oh, I can tell. And I agree that she probably followed your group. Maybe she heard about the bonfire and wanted to join you, make friends with the popular kids. Is that what happened?"

"What? No. We didn't know she even took that picture. I mean, we never saw her. We didn't know she was spying on us."

Shanna zoomed the photo. "That story doesn't fit what I see in this picture. You, Tristan Cargill and Jack Neal are all looking directly at the camera. You saw her."

"No. No, we didn't. We were just looking in that direction. It's a coincidence." Her knuckles were turning red and raw from rubbing and squeezing her hands together.

"Peyton," Kaden said. "What did you do when you and the others saw her taking your picture? Did you yell at her? Run after her?"

Peyton shook her head, looking down at her hands. "No. We didn't know she was there."

"This picture tells me otherwise."

Peyton looked away.

Kaden gave Peyton a hard look. "Did you chase her? Knock her down? Warn her that you'd hurt her if she ever followed you again?"

"No. I wouldn't do that. I'm not like that."

"What about one of the guys?" Shanna asked. "Sam Morton was a football player, big, intimidating. Maybe he got rough trying to scare her and knocked her around. I can see that. I'll tell Chief Dawson to bring Sam in for an interview and—"

"No. Don't. Sam's a good person. He'd never hit a

woman. He's not the one... He didn't..." She squeezed her hands harder.

"Ah, I see," Shanna said. "Tristan. Spoiled little rich kid beats up the annoying girl who dared to intrude on your little party in the woods. I can see him doing that and—"

"That's not what happened. Tristan didn't... I mean..." She swore beneath her breath.

Shanna exchanged a knowing look with Kaden. They were close to a break. She could feel it. "Peyton," she asked, "If it wasn't Sam, or Tristan, was it Jessica?"

"It was Jack, okay? There. I said it. He's the one who did it." She pressed a hand to her mouth, a horrified expression on her face as she dropped her face into her hands.

"What did he do?" Shanna went for the jugular, not giving Peyton a chance to regroup. "Did Jack beat her? Do something worse?"

When Peyton remained silent, Shanna nodded at Kaden, trying to let him know that she wanted them both to jump in and fire questions, increase the tension. They both did exactly that, taking turns, barely giving Peyton enough time to answer before asking another one. Kaden had a real knack for knowing where Shanna was heading and playing right along. He was the perfect Dr. Watson.

He tapped the bonfire photo again on Shanna's phone. "The date stamp on this tells us this was a week before your graduation. A few weeks before Tanya went missing. She didn't say anything to her parents about it. And they certainly didn't mention anything about bruises or cuts, no black eyes, so no one hit hurt. Not that anyone could see anyway. Peyton, what did he do that's so bad that you're afraid to tell us? Did he rape her?"

Peyton's head jerked up. "What? No, nothing like that.

It's just that…" She bit her lip, glancing back and forth between them with a panicked expression on her face. "None of us hit her or—or…did anything to her. We saw her taking the picture and Jack wanted to erase it. That's all. We—we were smoking weed, okay? Jack's the one who got it for us and he was scared he'd get in trouble with his parents if they found out. His dad would beat the crap out of him if he ever knew he did drugs. And the rest of us were worried she would show the picture to the cops. That's it. That's all."

But that wasn't all. Shanna could see that Peyton was still covering up something, hiding the full truth. It was obvious in the way she was wringing her hands, the tortured look in her eyes, how she could barely look at either of them. Shanna glanced at Kaden, and waited, letting him continue since he was doing so well.

He motioned toward the phone. "I don't see any drugs in that photo."

Peyton glanced at the screen, then looked away. "Maybe not that one. But there were others. Jack chased her down, took her phone, deleted everything. I mean *everything*. All her photos, not just the ones she took of us. She—she begged him not to, said she'd delete the ones of the bonfire. But he held the phone up to her face so it would unlock and he deleted everything in her photo app. And he warned her not to follow us ever again. I don't… I don't know how you got that picture. I thought they were all gone."

Shanna shook her head. "Maybe Tanya's just smarter than you and your friends. Haven't you ever gone to the recently deleted photo folder on your phone to recover pictures?"

Peyton's face reddened. "What are you talking about?"

Shanna sighed. "Never mind. What happened after Jack deleted the pictures?"

"I don't—"

"No more lies, Peyton. What happened after Jack caught up to Tanya?"

Her lower lip quivered. "Nothing. I mean, like I said, he warned her to stop following us around. She was a pest, you know? Always trying to talk to us at school, asking us over to her house, wanting to go shopping in Chattanooga with Jessica and me." She made a disgusted sound. "Like we'd ever do that."

Kaden stared at her. "You were upset at her for trying to be your friend?"

Peyton lifted her chin at a defiant angle. "You had to be there to understand. We weren't trying to be mean or anything. We just…had nothing in common with her, okay? She was a kid, a sophomore. I guess she was desperate or something, trying to fit in, and thought we could help her. She was trying to use us to become popular. It was ridiculous. She wouldn't stop. Just kept bugging us, following us around at school and—"

"She followed you again, didn't she?" Shanna asked. "After the bonfire, after Jack deleted those pictures and warned her. Was there another bonfire? More weed? Maybe the night she disappeared? And you caught her again?"

"Of course not." Peyton started to shake.

"She saw you illegally drinking alcohol?"

"No."

"Something worse? Heavy drugs? Meth?"

A single tear coursed down her cheek as she shook her head no.

"Peyton." Kaden took the lead again. "What did Tanya

see the night she went missing that she shouldn't have seen?"

She shook her head again. "It wasn't like that. That's not what—"

"Happened?"

She drew a ragged breath.

Shanna stared at her, waiting. But when Peyton remained silent, she nodded at Kaden to try again.

"You know where she is," he said, his voice kind but laced with steel. "Tell us."

Another tear spilled down her cheek and dropped to her lap. "You're wrong," she whispered, sounding desperate. "I don't know where she is. That's the honest truth."

Shanna glanced at Kaden. He shrugged, clearly unsure whether to believe the girl or not. He motioned for her to take it from here.

"But you do know what happened to her," Shanna pressed, her voice hard without any sympathy like Kaden's had been. This girl might very well be a murderer. Or she could be covering for someone who was. Shanna didn't feel an ounce of sympathy for her.

Peyton's eyes closed, her breaths coming in labored pants.

"She's dead, isn't she?" Shanna demanded.

"Oh, my God." Peyton covered her face in her hands, silent sobs shaking her shoulders.

Kaden winced, obviously pained at seeing the young woman so upset. He'd done an amazing job helping Shanna push Peyton to this point. But he wasn't the seasoned investigator that she was and appeared to have reached the end of his tolerance for playing the bad guy to Shanna's bad girl. He began to rise, as if to try to comfort Peyton. But Shanna put her hand on his and shook her head.

His jaw tightened, as if he was waging an internal battle. But he finally gave her a curt nod and settled back against the couch.

This time, it was Shanna who stood, moving to the other side of the coffee table and sitting on it across from Peyton. She covered the young woman's clasped hands with her own and leaned in close. It was time to take this to the finish line.

"Whatever happened, it's over, in the past. It can't be undone. But if you tell the truth, tell us where to find Tanya, we can at least bring her back to her family. Her parents need to know. They need to give their baby girl a proper burial."

Peyton choked on a sob.

"She was fifteen," Shanna whispered. "If you disappeared when you were only fifteen, don't you think your parents would deserve to know what happened? To know where you were?"

"Stop," Peyton pleaded. "Stop."

"The only one who can make this stop is you, by telling the truth. Tanya's parents need to find their baby girl. Where is she, Peyton? Where's Tanya?"

"I don't… I don't know where she is. I really don't." Her words were a ragged whisper, sounding as if they'd been wrenched from her soul.

"But you know what happened to her, what was *done* to her."

Silence.

"Is that why you don't want to tell us? Because it wasn't

Jack who hurt her? It was you, wasn't it? That's it. You hurt Tanya."

Peyton's head jerked up. "No. No, it wasn't me."

"Then who was it?"

Her lips trembled, her face so pale her skin seemed translucent. "All of us."

Shanna stilled, so shocked and dismayed that she couldn't respond.

Kaden came to her rescue, sitting beside her a few feet from the prom queen. "Peyton?" His voice was gentle, compelling, but somehow brooked no refusal in spite of that. "End this. Now. Tell us the truth. Who is *all of us*?"

Her face seemed to crumple as she answered. "Jack. Tristan. Jessica. Sam. And..." A fresh flood of tears flowed down her cheeks. "Me. We did it. All of us. We killed Tanya Jericho."

Chapter Fourteen

Shanna always hated this part of an investigation, the point where she had to involve the police and relinquish her control over the case she'd been working on. But at least Chief Dawson was letting her and Kaden sit in on Peyton's interview.

Not that he really had a choice.

For some reason, once Peyton had broken down and told Shanna and Kaden that she and her friends had killed Tanya, she'd clung to Shanna and sobbed on her shoulder. From that point on, Peyton had refused to let go of Shanna's hand. And she'd threatened to call a lawyer and not say anything else unless the police interviewed her at her home and allowed Kaden and Shanna to be there.

So now, Shanna sat on the couch beside Peyton, offering comfort to the girl who was apparently, at least partly, responsible for the death of the young girl they were trying to find. Sometimes life really sucked.

Across from her, Chief Dawson asked Peyton questions, with Officer Fletcher recording the session off to the side as unobtrusively as possible. Kaden sat beside Dawson, his gaze locked on Shanna most of the time, silently offering her the support that he seemed to instinctively know that she needed. She smiled her thanks, but then something that Peyton said had both her and Kaden looking at her in surprise.

Chief Dawson leaned forward, his forearms resting on his thighs. "Wait a minute. Now you're changing your story and saying you and your friends did *not* kill Tanya Jericho?"

"What? No. No, I'm just explaining what happened."

Shanna exchanged a quick look with Kaden, who shrugged, as confused as she was.

"Let's back up," Dawson said. "Two weeks after graduation, the third week of May and the night that Tanya Jericho went missing, you said she again followed you and your friends to one of the bonfires you liked to hold out in the woods by the lake."

"Yes. I've told you that like four times already."

"It's important to get this right. It's a different bonfire than the one in that picture that Ms. Hudson showed me, correct?"

Peyton clutched Shanna's hand more tightly. "Yes. This was a different one, the last bonfire we ever held because—because of what happened that night."

Dawson referred to his notes on the coffee table in front of him. "Got it. You were all five partying as in drinking and getting high on marijuana. You heard a noise and realized Tanya was watching you. That made you mad."

"Well, yes. Of course. We'd told her to stop following us around and spying. We'd all graduated by then and thought it was ridiculous for a kid to be following five adults around like a lost puppy."

The empathy Shanna had begun to feel for Peyton after she'd broken down earlier was rapidly drying up. Did the girl have no clue how bad she sounded? She'd admitted to murder and here she was, victim-blaming. The whole thing made Shanna want to pull her hand free and join Kaden on the other couch. But she couldn't risk doing anything that might stop the confession. They still needed the final clue, the location of Tanya's body.

Tension showed in the lines around Dawson's mouth as he continued to politely question Peyton. But his professionalism kept him from revealing any anger or disgust as he worked at getting the truth. "Where exactly was this last bonfire held?"

"In the woods, by the lake."

"Near where our divers have been searching? Where we found Tristan Cargill?"

She frowned. "No, of course not. I'll never understand why Tristan was found over there. All of us, including him, stayed on our side of town."

Dawson blinked, looking confused. "Where is our side of town?"

"You know, past the marina, but on the other side of the lake. On the same side as Stella's B and B but way down."

"So it's past the campground."

"A few miles past, yes. But—"

"On the other side of the lake. Got it. Is there a landmark you can give me?"

"I don't know about any landmarks right there, but it's past the Andersons' place and the mountain that looks like it's been split in two."

"Cooper's Bluff?"

"Yeah, yeah. That's it. Maybe a mile past that."

"All right. We'll get you a map in a bit and maybe you can show me. Let's get back to what you were saying earlier. At this bonfire, when you saw Tanya, Jack dragged her into the clearing by the fire. And the rest of you…spoke to her. Correct?"

Her hand squeezed Shanna's again. She was shaking, ever so slightly, her face pale. Maybe the way she was talking was more false bravado than lack of caring about her victim. Shanna squeezed back and Peyton gave her a grateful look, leaning into her side.

"Correct," Peyton said. "But you're—you're making it sound better than it was. We were mean, Chief Dawson. We said terrible, hurtful things. I'm not saying I wouldn't have said them sober, but I don't think me or the others would have been quite as…horrible if we weren't drinking and smoking."

"But no one hit her, or assaulted her in any way?"

She cleared her throat, her gaze falling to her lap. "Not at that point, no."

"Walk me through it, right up to where you said she was in the water. That's where you lost me earlier. After you had the shouting match by the bonfire, Tristan grabbed her and—"

"No. Tristan *shoved* her. His leg was hurt, remember? He was using a cane to walk so he couldn't grab her arm. He would have fallen. He bumped her, really. Hard. It was Jack who grabbed her and dragged her toward the lake."

"What did you and the others do when Jack was dragging her toward the water?"

"Well… Jessica, I think she was the least drunk of all of us. She was mad. At us. She kept telling us to leave Tanya alone. She hung back by the fire."

"But she didn't physically try to stop any of you, or help Tanya?"

"No." Her voice was quiet, sad. "Neither did I. I stopped at the edge of the water."

For the first time since she'd begun her confession, she sounded as if she felt ashamed of what she'd done.

Or what she hadn't done.

"Peyton," Dawson said. "This is important. Did all three of the boys—Tristan Cargill, Sam Morton and Jack Neal—did all three of them help pull Tanya into the water?"

"Yes," she whispered.

"And what did Tanya do?"

"She…" Peyton squeezed her eyes shut, all her earlier annoyance gone. It was as if she was finally facing the horror of what she and the others had done, and realizing just how awful they'd been.

"What did she do?" Dawson pressed.

"She was crying. She—she cried for her mom, asked them to let her go. She promised she'd never try to…try to be our friend again." Peyton let out a keening sob and covered her mouth. "Oh, my God. What did we do?"

"We'll take a break soon," Dawson said. "Hang in there. Once they got Tanya into the water, what happened next? Did they hold her under? Choke her? Hit her? What exactly did they do?"

She frowned, staring off into the distance as if trying to focus on the memories. "It all happened so fast. They pulled her out, pushed her. Then, she just disappeared."

Kaden exchanged another searching glance with Shanna. That's the part all of them were trying to understand.

"When you say pushed her," Dawson said. "Do you mean they pushed her head under the water?"

"No. No, nothing like that. They were trying to scare her. They reached one of those sharp drop-offs in the lake, about fifteen feet from shore. Then they just…pushed. She fell backward into the water and went under. That's it."

"She fell underneath the water and didn't come back up?"

"Exactly."

"Did anyone dive in to help her?"

Her chin wobbled. "We couldn't. We were drunk, high, scared. You know what happens at Mystic Lake. People go in and they don't come out. The lake took her. I swear we only wanted to scare her. But we killed her. She drowned, and it was our fault."

She broke down, crying again as she curled up against Shanna.

Shanna fought tears in her own eyes, hating this tug of war with her emotions. She hated what Peyton and her friends had done. But Peyton's anguish was real. She hated herself in that moment, and she was all alone in her grief and shame. Shanna wrapped her arms around her, whispering soothing words against the top of her head.

"I think it's time for that break," Kaden said.

Dawson nodded. "Agreed. I've got to get Jack Neal and Sam Morton into custody as quickly as possible before they compare notes and concoct some bogus story to try to cover what they've done. Peyton, you were seen at the restaurant when we found Jessica DeWalt. So were Sam and Jack. Until Mr. Rafferty called to tell me you were here, we'd tried to find all three of you and couldn't. Where did you all go after you left Stella's?"

Shanna gently helped Peyton to a sitting position and wiped the tears from her cheeks. "Where are Sam and Jack?"

"I—I don't know where they are. I heard about Tristan

and called them. We were upset and wanted to get together to talk about it. I couldn't… I couldn't get in touch with Jessica." She wiped the streaming tears from her eyes. "I don't understand what's happening around here."

"Did you meet with them at the restaurant?" Dawson asked. "I just need to know where they are."

"No. I mean yes. I…saw Mr. Rafferty carrying Jessica and I—I ran and found Sam and Jack. We agreed to meet in the woods behind the public boat ramp. We thought we were cursed, or something. I mean, how could that happen to Tristan and Jessica? It doesn't make sense, unless it's the universe getting back at us for being so horrible."

"You haven't seen them or heard from them since the boat ramp?"

"No. I heard the police, you, wanted to talk to me, so I—I hid until I thought you'd given up and then came home."

"All right." He checked his phone. "The time is seventeen thirty, five thirty in the afternoon. The first interview with Peyton Holloway is concluded." He motioned to Fletcher to turn off the camera.

"What happens now?" Peyton asked, sniffling and straightening on the couch.

Dawson pulled out a pair of handcuffs. "I need you to stand up and turn around."

ONCE PEYTON WAS in the back of Officer Fletcher's police car heading down the mountain, Kaden stood with Shanna and Chief Dawson by the chief's SUV.

"What's going to happen to Peyton?" Shanna asked.

"She'll be arraigned before a county judge, who will decide whether or not to set bail. However, even if she makes bail, I'd rather not let her out. Five friends and one wannabe friend go into the woods. Nearly a year later, most of those people are either missing or dead. Peyton is alive and unharmed so far and I want to keep her that way."

"You're talking protective custody?" Kaden asked.

"I am. I've issued a BOLO to neighboring law-enforcement agencies, be on the lookout, for Sam and Jack's vehicles. There's only one road in and out of this town, so I've got eyes on that, not to mention security cameras. But so far, there haven't been any sightings. We'll perform a cursory search of the boat ramp as soon as I leave. That's all we can do with the sun going down soon. A more thorough, organized search with local volunteers will take place tomorrow."

"Chief," Shanna said. "If you do find Jack Neal, there's something you should know. Kaden and I got a look earlier today at Tanya's last high-school yearbook. She'd defaced Jack's picture, adding devil horns and knives in his head. From what I've heard, she was a smart, sweet young girl. I can't imagine her doing that unless he'd done something really bad to her. I'm not sure if erasing the photos on her phone qualifies, like we told you earlier, especially since it appears that she was able to recover her pictures."

His jaw tightened. "I'll keep that in mind if I do get a chance to interview him. Is there anything else?"

"Not from me," she said.

"I've got a question," Kaden said. "I'm sure you have this covered already, but I have to ask. Do you have someone at the hospital guarding Jessica DeWalt, just in case there really is someone after all these kids?"

Dawson winced. "She didn't make it. Sorry. I know you both did everything you could to give her a chance. She passed away a couple of hours ago. I received the notification right before you called about Peyton and haven't had a chance to update you."

Kaden stared at him a long moment, shocked to hear about the girl's death. He gave Dawson a terse nod to thank him for the update.

Shanna leaned against his side, her arm around his back as if to let him know she was there for him. It was amazing how well she understood him. She obviously realized what a sucker punch it was to find out that the young woman he'd tried so hard to save hadn't been saved after all and was trying to offer him comfort. He glanced down at her, the burden in his chest lightening, if only a little, as he met her knowing, sympathetic gaze.

"I appreciate what you've both done to light a fire under this investigation," Dawson said. "I assure you it's no longer cold. It's all hands on deck. Shanna, take that vacation your sister promised. It might be hard to enjoy it at this point, but at least you can relax and chill out for a few days before you have to head back to West Virginia."

"What is it with all you police trying to get me to quit? I'm going to see this through until we bring Tanya home."

His jaw tightened. "I've got three young people dead now—Tanya, Tristan, and Jessica. And you have some crazy ex-boyfriend after you. I strongly recommend you go ahead and head back home, tonight. Get out of town. No one will think less of you. You've done what you could."

She put her hands on her hips. "I don't see you telling Kaden to tuck tail and run."

"That's because I'm selfish. I need his help."

"The search for Tanya's remains," Kaden said. "You want me to check the lake out past Cooper's Bluff with my sonar?"

"I'd sure appreciate it, if you're inclined to do so. I can't pull the Chattanooga dive team off the crime scene for Tristan Cargill just yet. They have to finish searching for additional bones and any evidence that might be at the scene. It could be days before they free up. Even then, there's no guarantee I'm next in line for additional dive-team assistance, not when the person I want them to dive for has been missing for nearly a year and we can't say for sure exactly where her remains might be. It sounds callous, I know, but they have to prioritize resources and have already spent a lot of time here in Mystic Lake. But if your fancy sonar finds something, they'll know it's not a wild goose chase and might help us that much sooner."

"When do you want to head out?"

"As soon as the mist burns off the lake tomorrow morning."

Kaden glanced at Shanna. "Are you leaving, as he suggested?"

"Hell, no."

He sighed. "I'll help you, Dawson. But only if you put Shanna in protective custody while I'm on the boat."

She gasped and pulled away from him. "No one's locking me up."

He faced her and put his hands on her shoulders. "I know the police didn't find any proof that Troy Warren has been near your sister's cabin. But I'm not willing to risk your safety if he's just good at covering his tracks. I'm assuming the worst, that he's here, somewhere in Mystic Lake. I'm not leaving you alone."

"Kaden, I can take care of myself. I—"

"She can join us on the boat," Dawson said. "I plan on going with you as your backup. No one should ever swim or dive in Mystic Lake without someone around to help if something goes sideways—as it often does around here. Two people to back you up is even better. Shanna can call for help while I dive in after you if necessary."

"Okay," Shanna said, her face pale in spite of her brave words.

"No," Kaden countered, still holding Shanna. "Not happening. There's no way you're getting back on my boat. It was hard enough for you last time, especially with how the trip ended. I'm not going to put you through that again. We already know how this trip will end, if we're lucky. It'll end in the discovery of more remains."

Dawson looked at Shanna, his confusion evident. "If you're worried about seeing a dead body, keep in mind we're talking bones at this point."

Shanna started to speak again but Kaden cut her off. "Her reasons are personal. She's not getting back on my boat. Period."

She shoved his hands off her shoulders. "Isn't that my decision?"

"No."

She raised her hands in the air and rolled her eyes.

Dawson smiled. "Okay, none of my business. I get it. But, there's a simple solution. Shanna, if you won't leave town or let me put you in a holding cell for your protection, there's someone else who can look after you while we're on the boat. Aidan O'Brien, Grace's husband. Trust me. No one's going to mess with Aidan. You'll be completely safe with him at your sister's cabin."

Kaden shook his head. "I don't like it. I've never met the guy. You may trust him, but I don't."

"Um, hello." Shanna waved her arms in the air again.

"Quit talking about me as if I'm not here. This isn't either of your decisions. It's mine." She turned to Kaden. "I appreciate you being okay with me not getting back on your boat. Since Chief Dawson is going to be your backup, I'll agree to that. But as for my protection, I'm a big girl. Have you forgotten I have a gun?" She glanced at the chief. "That's okay, I hope? I didn't even think about checking the Tennessee laws on gun ownership before coming here."

Dawson smiled. "We live in the wilderness with bears and so-called phantoms roaming the woods." He winked. "I'd be surprised if any adults living around here *don't* have a gun."

She nodded. "That settles it."

"No," Kaden said. "It doesn't."

She pressed a hand against his chest. "Kaden, your protectiveness is sweet and I really appreciate that you care. But you're going overboard with this. The police don't think Troy is in town. Even if he is, I'll be just fine by myself in Cassidy's cabin. Chief, I appreciate you suggesting that Mr. O'Brien can protect me. But I'd feel awkward with someone I don't know there and honestly don't feel it's necessary."

The chief shrugged, appearing weary of arguing anymore.

"Shanna," Kaden began again, "I don't want—"

"It's not what you do or don't want that matters this time. I really can take care of myself. And something you don't realize is that Cassidy has real working shutters on all her windows. Solid wood to keep out dangerous storms, or bears. Thick enough to stop a bullet, just like the walls... as we both know."

Dawson frowned in confusion again.

Kaden reluctantly smiled. "Yes. We do."

"I'll be okay, really. I'll be locked up tight where I'm comfortable and can make myself useful with my laptop and the investigative folders to continue looking into the case. Someone is after Peyton and her crew. If I can help come up with a list of potential suspects, then that's what I'm going to do."

"I really don't want you there alone," Kaden told her.

"And I don't want the Jerichos to wait days or weeks for the Chattanooga dive team to find their daughter. I want this over with before we both have to go back to our respective businesses. Please. Trust me. While you help in your way, I'll help in mine. Okay?"

"You'll stay inside? Locked up tight, no matter what? No going into town to conduct interviews?"

"I won't open the door until I hear your voice. Even if I think Troy's out snooping in the woods, I won't go looking for him. Shooting him would just result in more paperwork for our friend Dawson."

Dawson chuckled. "Thanks. I think."

Kaden shook his head. "You're really something, you know that?"

"So I'm told."

He squeezed her hand, then faced Dawson. "I'll do it. I'll take the boat out, work with the sonar."

Relief flashed across Dawson's face. "Thanks. Thank you both."

"How big of a search area are we talking about?" Kaden asked. "Any idea?"

"Too big to search without narrowing it down. I asked Fletcher to work with Peyton at the station, get her to mark the target area on a map. Hopefully, she'll cooperate. As soon as I've got some coordinates, I'll text them to you so you can plan your approach. Your boat is still docked at the Tate cabin, right?"

"It is."

"I'll meet you there in the morning once we have those coordinates. My police SUV parked outside will be yet another deterrent against anyone up to no good." He hopped into his SUV. "Kaden, is that your Lexus parked down the road?"

"It's mine," Shanna said.

"Hop in. I'll take you to it."

Chapter Fifteen

Shanna turned from the kitchen sink as Kaden stepped inside the cabin with his overnight bag. He immediately shut and locked the door, then surprised her by sliding one of the kitchen chairs under the doorknob.

She tossed the dishcloth she'd been using onto the counter, having just finished cleaning up from their dinner. "Paranoid much?"

"I'm getting that way." He set his bag down on the table.

"Something happen while you were getting your stuff from your boat?" She looked toward the front windows, then remembered that he'd insisted on shutting and locking all of the shutters over them when they'd first arrived and after he'd searched the tiny cabin to make sure that Troy, the Phantom, or any other possible bad guy wasn't inside. "What is it?" She glanced at the covered windows again, starting to feel uneasy. "Did you see someone outside?"

"I checked the perimeter before coming in. It seems to be all clear." He shoved his hands in his pants pockets. "Dawson called. As expected, the initial search of the public boat ramp down the road from Stella's came up empty. No sign of Sam or Jack."

"Hopefully they're safe and just hiding out somewhere like we talked about. What about Peyton? Did she narrow down the area where they had that last bonfire? Will you and Dawson be able to take the boat out in the morning to search for Tanya?"

"She cooperated, gave a specific location. Dawson's meeting me here around nine."

"That's good news."

"Yes." His expression was tense, in spite of what he'd said.

"Kaden? Is something else going on?" She pressed a hand to her chest. "Did Dawson…did they find another body?"

He shook his head, then slowly crossed the room, stopping so close to her that she had to tilt her head back to look him in the eyes.

"Kaden? What's wrong? You're worrying me."

He drew a ragged breath but didn't say anything.

She frowned in confusion. She'd never seen him this way, so tense, so…keyed up. Then again, they hadn't known each other all that long. And how was that possible when she felt as if she'd known him forever? They'd been together almost 24/7 since the moment they'd met, spending far more time than if they'd been casually dating for weeks, or months. Maybe that's why she felt so in tune with him. And yet, this morose, tense man standing before her was a side of Kaden she'd never seen. She didn't understand his mood, or know what had caused it.

She touched his chest to get him to look at her.

He jerked as if she'd branded him, giving her his full attention. Slowly, ever so slowly, he placed his hands on either side of her against the countertop, trapping her with his body, his heat, his jaw so tense he seemed to be in pain. And then, she knew. She understood.

Her pulse quickened, her belly tightened deliciously as she slid her fingers across his shirt over his heart. It was pounding just as fast as hers. He was a man on edge, struggling for control.

She smiled.

He swore even as he feathered his hand across her cheek, sending a shiver down her spine. That slow caress continued down the side of her neck. Her skin flushed hot and cold everywhere he touched. Since when had her neck ever been that sensitive?

His throat worked as he leaned down, closer, his mouth angling toward hers. She stood on tiptoe to meet him halfway. Suddenly he let her go, swearing again as he strode away from her, stopping in front of one of the shuttered windows beside the couch.

She blinked in surprise and settled back on her feet. Disappointment and confusion warred with each other as she pushed away from the kitchen counter and followed him. "What was that about?"

He slowly turned around, his hands shoved in his pockets as if to keep himself from reaching for her. His eyes had darkened to the color of midnight and practically blazed with heat. "Do you have any idea how beautiful you are?"

Her breath caught at the hungry look in his eyes, the rough rasp in his voice. Her pulse began to race, her belly tightening with desire. It was a heady feeling, knowing he wanted her as much as she'd been wanting him for what felt like forever. But she'd just embarrassed herself by responding when it seemed that he was going to kiss her. She wasn't putting herself out there again. The ball was in his court. It was up to him now.

He drew a ragged breath, then shook his head. "I'm sorry.

I know I'm being a jerk. I don't mean to be, I just…do you have any clue how utterly frustrating it is that we're both going to sleep in the same tiny cabin tonight and knowing I shouldn't touch you?"

She had to curl her hands at her sides to keep from reaching for him. "Shouldn't? Why?"

He frowned, as if the answer was obvious. "Why? I live in Charleston. My business is there."

"So?"

His frown deepened. "You live in West Virginia."

"Yes. And? What's the problem?"

"What's the problem? Seriously? Our businesses, our livelihoods, are a day's drive apart. We could never be… It wouldn't make sense to… Ah, hell." He yanked his hands free and scrubbed his face that was already showing signs of needing a shave. "I'm sorry. This is… I never should have said anything. I was just sitting on my boat and thinking about you here, and me, tonight, and I couldn't… I wanted… Damn. I'm trying to be a gentleman."

She took a step closer, then another, until her breasts pushed against his chest.

His Adam's apple bobbed in his throat as his gaze dipped down.

"Kaden?"

He shuddered and seemed to struggle to force his gaze up until he was looking at her face. "Shanna?"

The way his voice caressed her name had her flushing hot all over. This time, she was the one who traced the outline of his cheek, feathered her hands down the side of his neck, then across his lips. A bead of sweat ran down his cheek even though it was cool inside the cabin.

"Shanna, I don't… It wouldn't be right to start…something between us that has no future. You get that, right? I don't want to hurt you, or treat you with anything but respect. You deserve to be protected, cherished, not used for a night when there's no possibility of a future relationship."

She stared up at him, searching his smoldering gaze. "You want me."

He swallowed. "Yes."

"And I want you."

His nostrils flared, but he remained silent.

"But you're holding back because you feel I deserve respect, and to be…cherished?"

His hand shook as he reached for her. Then his fingers curled against his palm and he dropped his hand to his side without touching her. "You deserve so much more than I can ever give you."

She stared at him in wonder. "Wow. Why couldn't I have met you when I was sixteen?"

He frowned. "Sixteen?"

"When I was a champion swimmer with a gazillion swim-meet medals to my name. Did I ever tell you that?"

He slowly shook his head. "No. I thought you were terrified of the water."

"I am. But back then, I wasn't. I loved the water, swimming, diving, anything I could do to feel it rush through my fingers as I pulled myself forward faster and faster. I wanted to be an Olympic champion. But it wasn't meant to be." She cupped his cheek in her hand, unable to resist the desire to touch, to treasure.

To cherish.

"What happened?" His dark eyes searched hers, the desire tempered with concern.

Because he cared about her.

It was a heady knowledge to have.

She slowly slid her hand down the side of his neck, as he'd done to her earlier, delighting at the feel of his pulse speeding up beneath her fingertips.

"For my sixteenth birthday, my parents threw a pool party at our home and invited all my friends. Once everyone left, I was in the pool getting all of the floats out, when one of my friend's brothers who'd come with her to the party suddenly appeared in our backyard. He'd made advances earlier. But I told him I wasn't interested."

Kaden's eyes darkened, the heat tinged with anger as he gently took her hand in his. "Please tell me he didn't… that he didn't—"

"Attack me?"

He nodded.

"He kissed me, or tried to. But I turned my head and told him to leave. The rest of it happened so fast I don't remember all the details. He…shoved me under the water, grabbed my breast. I kicked and swam away. But he was a strong swimmer, too. He dove, pinned me to the bottom of the pool, yanked down my bikini bottoms and…" She drew a shaky breath. "I haven't spoken about this to anyone besides my parents. And the police. And my therapist. Ever. Not even with my little sister, Cassidy."

His hand was shaking now as he held hers, his thumb gently rubbing her palm in a soothing motion. "And you don't have to tell me this, either. I don't want you to relive something so awful."

"I want to tell you. I want you to understand. He didn't… The boy didn't do what he wanted. My dad saw him from the kitchen window and dove into the pool. He jerked him off me and hauled him out. That's when it happened."

He frowned, his thumb stopping its soothing motions against her palm. "What happened?"

She drew a bracing breath before continuing. "When I pushed off the bottom of the pool to swim to the surface, my hair got caught in the drain. I don't think that would happen in a modern pool, but it was an old house, with an old pool. My hair was long and…well, I woke up in the hospital. My dad had realized what was happening and grabbed a knife from the kitchen to free me. I don't remember that part. I'd lost consciousness by then. But I do remember waking up with a really bad haircut."

She chuckled but he didn't smile back. His expression was a mixture of anger, shock and sympathy.

"That's why you're afraid of the water," he said.

"Apparently. I haven't been able to get near it since without feeling nauseous. My therapist at the time told me it was like riding a horse, that I needed to hop back on to get over my fear. But every time I tried… I couldn't. So I gave it up. I never went near a pool again."

"Please tell me the jerk who attacked and almost killed you got what was coming to him."

"We had a security camera that caught everything. But I didn't want to go to court, be victimized all over again. I'm sure his lawyer would have made me out to be some temptress or something equally stupid to justify his client's actions. We settled out of court, kept it quiet, even though I promise you my dad wanted to kill him." She smiled. "But that's not why I told you. I told you because I trust you enough to tell you the worst thing that ever happened to me. Well, aside from Troy. He's the second worst thing to happen to me. But that's different. And I don't even want to go there right now. Kaden, you say I deserve to be protected, cherished. You make me feel that way, already, just by being here, wanting to keep me safe. And by denying yourself something I would freely give, because you care about me. You're worried that it will hurt me to spend a night in your arms when there's no possibility of a future relationship. But isn't that my decision to make?"

"Shanna—"

"We don't know what the future holds. But I do know how I feel tonight, right now. I care about you, too. Hold me, Kaden. Cherish me. Make me forget everything else if only for a night. Erase the hurts, the pain, the struggles. Love me, Kaden. Even if one night is all we ever have."

He made a strangled sound deep in his throat. Then she was in his arms, cradled against his chest as he carried her into the bedroom.

Chapter Sixteen

We're here. Dawson's getting ready to head back to town.

Shanna read Kaden's text then tossed her phone onto the kitchen table and jumped up to put her shoes on. Last night in Kaden's arms had been incredible. Saying goodbye this morning had been torture. Waiting all day, closed up in the cabin with just her investigative folders and the internet to keep her company, had been a study in boredom. Normally an investigation got her excited, pumped. But she'd grown used to Kaden being around. Without him, she'd been…lost.

What that meant to her future happiness once they parted wasn't something she even wanted to contemplate. After all, Kaden had warned her. She knew there was no future for them, and agreed that giving up their businesses and moving wasn't going to happen. But that didn't make it any less hard to even think about saying goodbye.

Which was why she refused to think about it right now.

She shoved that unpleasant thought to the back of her mind and hurried out the front door and down the porch steps to the side where the vehicles were parked. She had a big smile on her face for Kaden. But his back was to her and it was Chief Dawson who saw her first. His eyes widened, then he grinned knowingly as she forced herself to slow her bouncy steps and dim her smile.

"Hello, Shanna. Good to see you again."

"Chief." She barely managed a nod before heading to Kaden. She stopped a few feet away as he turned around.

His mouth curved in a sexy, glad-to-see-you smile. "Hey, there."

"Hey, yourself. I thought you, um, both of you would never be done with your search. How did it go?"

His smile faded. "Not too well. But it wasn't a complete bust."

"What do you mean?"

He motioned toward Dawson.

Dawson leaned back against his SUV. "We found the clearing that Peyton described. Apparently, her group isn't the only one that has bonfires out there. I'm guessing the current senior class does as well since there are plenty of signs of recent activity. Finding something of evidentiary value there is a nonstarter. But it does corroborate Peyton's story, which helps with building a chargeable case. But Kaden's sonar search didn't come up with anything, not for lack of trying. He scanned all over that cove and ended up diving for several hours to check out some of the structures under the water in case sediment had covered up any remains."

"What? Kaden, you dove into the debris? Isn't that one of the main things people say is deadly in that lake?"

Dawson winced. "Didn't mean to get you in hot water, buddy."

"I was careful." He shrugged. "It had to be done. And I'm going back tomorrow. Tanya has to be there. We know we're searching the right place. But it's a difficult area to search. The sonar isn't working its magic. It could take days, maybe longer. I'll help as long as I can. But I have to get back to my company by the weekend. Dawson's going to put in a request to the Chattanooga dive team if I'm not able to find her before I leave."

Shanna wanted to ask him not to go back. But the reality was that part of the reason she was so drawn to him was because he was such a decent man. He was losing money being here when he could have been working for a paying customer in Charleston. And he was donating his time, and lost income, because he felt it was the right thing to do. How could she fault him for that? Or be angry? Or ask him to reconsider? Instead, she'd have to trust his expertise and experience to do what needed to be done without getting injured. Or worse.

Maybe she'd call Dawson in a private moment and put the fear of Shanna into him if he didn't make sure that Kaden came back unscathed from his diving trips.

Dawson exchanged an uneasy look with Kaden.

Shanna glanced back and forth between them. "What? There's something else?"

Kaden nodded. "The reports coming back from the search at the public boat ramp aren't encouraging. Sam and Jack weren't found, but their cars were. They'd been parked deep in the woods, off a trail. Dawson's theory is that they were forced against their will to go with someone through the woods to the road and taken away in another vehicle."

Shanna's stomach churned at the news. "Someone's after all of them isn't he? Peyton's little clique of friends."

"It's getting nearly impossible to think anything else is happening. The question is who, why, and how do we stop them?" Dawson glanced at the sky overhead. "We've got a couple more hours of daylight. The state police are bringing in lights and more dog teams to help search through the night. I'm heading over there once I leave. We have to find those boys before they end up like DeWalt and Cargill." He shook his head. "This just keeps getting worse and worse. And once the public hears about Peyton and the others and their involvement in Tanya's murder, they'll be putting a paranormal spin on this whole dang thing which will only make our jobs more difficult."

"What do you mean?" Shanna asked. "Blame it on the so-called Phantom?"

"That's one possibility. But I can see them saying that Tanya's spirit is haunting the lake, taking its revenge. That's exactly the kind of story the local kids like to spread around. Everything bad that happens here is blamed on the lake. If I don't find the guy responsible for the murders and disappearances, this episode will go down as yet another part of the legends that overshadow this town." He straightened away from his car. "You two be careful, just in case that Warren guy ends up making an appearance. With the run of bad luck we're having right now, it wouldn't surprise me."

As Dawson's SUV headed down the road, Kaden scanned the woods around the cabin.

"Stop worrying," Shanna said. "Troy may be a bully but he's also a coward. He's not going to hang around with a policeman close by. Or big, strong Kaden Rafferty."

He gave her a lopsided grin that had her pulse leaping.

"Big, strong Kaden Rafferty isn't going take a chance, either way," he teased. "Let's get you into the cabin behind a locked door. I want to hear about your progress on the investigation. Got any new leads?"

She grimaced. "Not really. The main thing I've been able to do is rule people out, not in. My potential suspect list is woefully short." She turned to jog up the stairs.

"Shanna! Get down!" Kaden yelled.

She dropped to the ground just before a bright flash of light zipped past her. She stared in shock at the haft of a large knife sticking out of the railing near where she'd been standing.

A loud bang had her whirling around, still on the ground.

"Get in the cabin," Kaden yelled. "Now."

He was on the ground a few yards away, wrestling with a man holding a gun.

"Shanna, go!" Kaden yelled, slamming an elbow against the side of the man's head.

Her fight-or-flight reflexes finally kicked in as she recognized whom Kaden was fighting.

Her ex. Troy Warren.

She took off, leaping up the stairs two at a time, her shoes squeaking on the wood as she slammed against the doorframe, going too fast to make the turn. She grunted at the pain and bolted into the cabin.

The sound of another gunshot outside had her cringing and praying that Kaden was okay. She grabbed her gun from her purse and ran outside, rushing down the steps, not even slowing down as she sprinted toward where the men were rolling around on the ground, close to Kaden's truck now.

Kaden threw a punch that slammed against Troy's jaw. Blood flew from his mouth, but he didn't stop wrestling for control of the gun.

Shanna stopped a few yards away, pointing her gun skyward, waiting for a clear shot.

Kaden caught sight of her and swore.

The distraction cost him.

Troy slammed an elbow against Kaden's face, and jerked the gun around toward him.

Shanna didn't have a clear shot, but she couldn't wait. She fired up in the air. *Bam! Bam!*

Troy screamed and threw himself against a truck tire.

Kaden grabbed his wrist and wrenched it up against the truck's frame.

Troy screamed again, blood gushing from where the frame had sliced his wrist. The gun went skittering across the ground.

As Kaden scrabbled forward to grab it, Troy took off toward the woods, cradling his wounded hand.

Shanna lowered her gun, lining up the sights at Troy's back. Just as she was about to squeeze the trigger, the gun was plucked from her grip.

Kaden swore. "What are you trying to do? Send yourself to prison over that sleazeball?"

She blinked, then blew out a shaky breath. "I wasn't thinking."

"Damn straight, you weren't. You should have stayed in the cabin, not offered yourself as a target. You took ten years off my life when you came back out here."

She put her hands on her hips. "A simple thank-you would be fine, instead of a lecture."

His swear-laced reply had her gasping in outrage. "Kaden Rafferty. How dare you—"

His mouth came down hard against hers as he pushed her back against the side of the cabin. He ravaged her mouth, setting her nerve endings on fire like molten lava. She whimpered deep in her throat and grasped his shirt, desperately trying to pull it free from his pants.

He broke away, swearing again. "You're dangerous."

"You're a tease."

"For the love of… Get in the cabin, Shanna. Call the police and—"

The sound of a siren had both of them looking down the road.

Shanna crossed her arms. "Looks like Dawson heard the shots."

"Good." He handed her gun back to her. "You can unlock the door once he gets here. In the meantime, barricade yourself inside. Warren's wounded but he's not down for the count."

He checked the loading of Warren's gun, then took off toward the woods, where he'd disappeared.

"Kaden, don't you dare go into those woods on your own. Let the police handle it."

He made a disgusted sound and jogged into the forest.

In desperation, Shanna yelled, "Don't you dare leave me alone to face some murderous psychopath while you go off chasing my idiot ex!"

Silence.

Then, Kaden slowly stepped out from the trees, his jaw set and the gun down at his side.

Dawson's SUV slid across the gravel driveway, barely stopping a few feet from Kaden's truck.

Kaden ignored him as he stalked forward to where Shanna stood at the bottom of the steps. "You don't play fair," he accused.

"As long as you're safe, that's what matters."

"Kaden, Shanna, what's going on? I heard gunshots." Dawson ran up to them, his weapon out and down at his side. "What happened?"

Kaden stared at Shanna and shook his head in disgust. "You do realize he almost killed you, right? And now, he's free to try again."

"Who's free to try again?" Dawson demanded.

Shanna smiled up at Kaden. "I have faith in you. You'll keep me safe."

Dawson rolled his eyes and stepped away to make a call. "Ortiz, yeah, I'm at the Tate cabin. Someone's been here shooting up the place. A knife's buried in one of the porch railings and there's blood and evidence of a scuffle beside Kaden's truck. I need backup… Yesterday. I'll update you on the situation and who we're after just as soon as I can get Kaden and Shanna to stop flirting with each other and answer my questions."

Kaden glared his displeasure at Dawson.

Shanna burst out laughing.

"At least tell me how many bad guys I'm after," Dawson said. "And which way they went."

Kaden arched an eyebrow at Shanna. "I've got backup. Now, will you lock yourself inside the cabin?"

"What?" Dawson asked. "I'm not backup. You are."

"I'd be happy to," she said. "Go get him." She jogged up the steps and headed into the cabin, locking the door behind her.

It couldn't have been more than fifteen minutes later when a knock sounded at the door.

"Ms. Hudson, it's Officer O'Brien."

Shanna hurried to unlock the door and pull it open. But

her greeting died on her lips when she saw the urgency in O'Brien's face. "What happened? Is Kaden—"

"Mr. Rafferty and the chief are both okay. The chief phoned in an update as I was pulling into the driveway. You're going to be hearing a lot more sirens, other people arriving, in just a few minutes. I've been asked to make sure you don't leave this cabin, that you stay locked inside. Even if, um, even if I have to handcuff you to the refrigerator, or whatever I can find to make sure you can't leave the cabin. Ma'am." Her face turned a slight red.

Shanna narrowed her eyes. "The chief wouldn't have told you that."

"Not in those words, no."

"Kaden did."

O'Brien gave her a pained smile. "Will you promise you'll wait until Mr. Rafferty or one of us police tell you it's okay to come out before you do so? Please?"

Shanna sighed. "Fine. Okay. I promise I won't come out until I'm given permission." She rolled her eyes. "But only if you swear that Kaden's really okay."

"He's uninjured, from what I've been told. I haven't seen him yet. I only spoke to him on the phone."

"Fair enough."

The policewoman gave her a relieved smile, then hurried outside, pulling the door closed behind her.

Shanna turned the lock, then settled down to wait, her foot tapping an impatient tune against the wooden floor.

"WAKE UP, BEAUTIFUL. We're leaving."

"Hmm?" Shanna slapped at the hand pulling on her covers and snuggled into her pillow.

An impatient sigh sounded. "Come on, sleepyhead. Your chariot awaits."

"Chariot?" She yawned, wondering what kind of dream had chariots and grumpy-sounding princes in them.

"Unbelievable," her prince complained.

Her world suddenly tilted and her head fell back against something hard. And warm. The ground began to shake. She grabbed for her pillow.

"Ouch, dang. Sheathe those claws." Her world tilted again and her bottom pressed down on something hard and cold.

Her eyes flew open. She blinked and looked around. What the? She was in the bathroom? On the floor?

"Ew," she exclaimed, trying to jump to her feet. Her legs got all tangled up in her comforter. Her comforter?

Laughter sounded above her.

She looked up into Kaden's amused eyes as he bent down and began pulling the comforter off her shoulders.

"Kaden?"

"Shanna?" He freed her and tossed the comforter into the tub.

"Why am I in the bathroom, on the floor? With you?"

"Because I couldn't wake you up. Do you always sleep like the dead?"

"I have no idea. Help me up. Why were you trying to wake me, anyway? Wait, Kaden. You're here."

He was laughing as he helped her stand. "I don't remember you being this confused this morning when you woke up."

"That's because I woke up on my own, not when some rude person dropped me onto the bathroom floor. Gross, by the way, regardless of how much of a clean freak my sister might be."

"I didn't drop you. And you have approximately five minutes to do whatever you need to do in here before we leave."

"Leave. Wait, that's what the prince said."

He frowned. "Prince?"

Her face heated. "Never mind. It must be late or I wouldn't be this tired. Not that I can tell the time with all the windows blocked out." She blinked at him, her stomach clenching with sympathy. "Your right eye's turning black."

"Warren got a lucky shot in earlier. Poor jerk."

"Poor jerk? He's a stalker and an attempted murderer. I have absolutely no sympathy for him. Wait. You caught him? Dawson's taking him to jail?"

His jaw tightened. "Not exactly." He glanced at his dive watch. "I'll explain on the way. I've already packed you a bag. Just…wash your face or whatever you need to do and get dressed. You have four more minutes. After that, I'm hauling you out of here, even if you're naked." He checked his watch. "Make that three minutes."

"Ugh." She stomped her feet in frustration and shooed him away with her hands. "Get out. I need a minute."

"I figured you would." He smiled, but it didn't quite reach his eyes, or ease the tension along his jaw.

Before she could ask him again what had happened, he left, pulling the door closed behind him.

True to Kaden's threat, he was back to get her in just a few minutes. Luckily she'd already emptied her bladder and brushed her teeth. She was tying her shoes when he knocked, then shoved open the door.

"Let's go."

She called him some unsavory names that had his mouth twitching with amusement, but he didn't complain. He didn't say anything at all. He just grabbed her hand, and hauled her through the cabin and out the door, barely giving her a chance to grab her purse.

The sky was black as velvet, not a star in sight. Clouds must have moved in while she was sleeping. Seeing the driveway and yard empty now, except for Kaden's truck, her sedan, and his boat trailer sitting near the end of the cabin sent a shiver up her spine. It was too dark, too quiet, especially given the chaos she'd heard outside earlier when all the police had been there.

Refusing to answer any questions, he lifted her into the truck and shut the door. After rushing around the hood, he hopped into the driver's seat, tossed a black leather carry-on bag into the back and locked his door. His tires spit gravel as he turned around in the yard, then he sent his truck barreling down the road toward town.

"Slow down, Mario Andretti," she complained, clinging to the armrest, "or we'll end up in a ditch."

He checked the rearview mirror and the side one before easing up slightly on the gas.

"Well, that was fun," she said, letting her death grip on the armrest go. "Fastest I ever got ready. Hope you don't mind the lack of makeup. Lucky for you I have some in my purse so I won't scare everyone who sees me in the morning. It's too late for me not to scare you."

As if against his will, his mouth curved in a smile. "You're adorable when you first wake up. But your disposition could use some sweetening."

She snorted.

He laughed.

"Since this is the road into town," she said, "and according to the clock in your truck it's past, oh wow, two thirty in the morning, we're either going to the police station—"

"Nope."

"Or…out of town?"

"Too far a drive right now through a creepy, dark two-lane road for an hour to reach Chattanooga. I'm half-asleep myself. We'll figure out our next steps in the morning, after we get some rest and both have a clear head."

"Ah. We're going to Stella's, the B and B."

"Best hotel in town."

"The only hotel in town."

He smiled. "I called ahead. The desk clerk said he'd leave our room key under the cookie jar on the counter."

"That sounds really secure."

"I'll clear the room before we go inside. And the police station is just across the lake. If we need them, they're less than a minute away."

"You sound like a cop yourself lately. 'Clear the room.' I think you've been around far too many police officers this week."

"I couldn't agree more."

"All right. The B and B. We've got about fifteen minutes before we get there. Well, the way you're driving, maybe only ten. Plenty of time for you to tell me what happened after I humored you by locking myself in the cabin. Speak, Kaden. I'm about out of patience."

By the time he made the turn at the end of Main Street and headed around the end of the lake in town, she was numb with shock over what he'd told her.

He and Dawson had tracked Troy into the woods and found him tied to a tree, his throat slit.

Beside him was Sam Morton. Tied to the same tree, covered in blood. But it wasn't his. It was Troy's. Sam had numerous cuts and scrapes, and was covered in bug bites. But there was nothing more serious wrong with him, physically at least, except for stun-gun burns on his neck.

Just like Jessica.

He'd seen the killer slice Troy's throat and was hysterical and blubbering behind a gag over his mouth when Dawson and Kaden found him.

When they'd calmed Sam down, he told them he and Jack had been taken at knifepoint and with the threat of a stun gun by the killer behind the public boat ramp, as the police had theorized. He'd forced them to hike endlessly through the mountains. Eventually, he'd brought them to a side-by-side, a four-wheeler hidden in the woods. He'd tied them to the seats and blindfolded them before taking them on a long, winding ride that seemed to take hours.

Sam didn't know where Jack was. Jack had been taken away while Sam was left handcuffed to a tree. This morning the killer brought Sam to the woods behind Cassidy's cabin. He'd heard in town that Shanna had some stalker bully after her. In his own sick way, the killer had planned to kill Sam—someone he considered to be a bully, too—and leave him as an offering of justice for Shanna.

When Troy showed up, he became the perfect target. Instead of killing Sam, the killer had murdered Troy. After slicing Troy's throat, he'd warned Sam, "This is what happens to bullies." Then he'd taken off before Kaden and Dawson could catch him.

Shanna shivered as Kaden pulled the truck into a parking space behind the B and B.

True to his word, the clerk had left the key under the

cookie jar. And Kaden, with a gun in his hand that must have been given to him by Dawson, made her wait just inside the door while he checked out the huge walk-in dressing room closet, under the bed, the attached bathroom—anywhere he thought a killer could possibly hide. Only then did he allow her to move freely around the room.

She immediately sank onto the bench at the end of one of the two double beds, her horrified and confused mind full of questions. But she only asked one.

"Kaden."

"Hmm." He'd just finished putting their toiletries in the bathroom and set the bag on a chair in the dressing room before sitting beside her.

"Who is this man who exacts his own form of perverted justice against people that he thinks are bullies? Who is he?"

His voice was subdued, tired, as he answered. "He told Sam he was the Phantom."

"Oh, my God." Her shoulders began to shake with her sobs as the events of the last few days shredded her composure.

Kaden pulled her onto his lap and cradled her, whispering soothing words against the top of her head as she cried against his neck.

Chapter Seventeen

Kaden listened to Dawson on the phone as he stood at the B and B's bedroom window, watching the sun come up over the lake trying to burn through the heavier-than-usual mist rising from the water.

"Sounds like a depressing lack of progress." Kaden tried to focus in spite of his right eye having swelled half-shut from that one lucky punch Warren had landed. "I'd have figured with the state police searching for Jack through the night that they'd have at least found some indication of where he might have been taken."

"Give me a break. Last time we saw each other was only, what, five hours ago? No, they haven't found Jack and, yes, they're still searching. Their search is focused on two areas now, the woods behind the boat ramp and behind the Tate cabin. But so far, no dice. Did you even get any sleep last night?"

"Not much." He glanced toward the bathroom as the door opened and Shanna came out, her hair damp from her shower and her body wrapped in one of the B and B's fluffy white towels. His mouth went dry as he watched her cross the room. With a sleepy smile and a wave, she headed into the large closet to get dressed.

"Kaden? Kaden, you still there?" Dawson asked.

"What? Oh, sorry. I was…distracted."

Dawson laughed. "I'll bet you were. How's Shanna doing?"

"What you'd expect. She was upset last night but she's strong. She's more determined than ever to find some kind of evidence today that will tell her where Jack's being held. She was combing through topography maps on her laptop before I even woke up, trying to figure out—in her words—where she'd hold someone captive if she was trying to hide in these mountains."

"More power to her. Have her pass along any theories she comes up with."

"Will do." Kaden leaned closer to the window. "The mist doesn't seem to be burning off as quickly as usual. Seems strange, given the warmer spring temperatures."

"They don't call it Mystic Lake just because of the mystical stories about it. That mist has a mind of its own. You never know when it will roll in or roll out. Are you okay staying at Stella's for a few more hours, at least until I get a safe house lined up and transport arranged? I sure don't want her out roaming around with this killer on the loose. He's got some weird thing about bullies and I don't know whether his sick offering yesterday is his only interest in her."

"She's not going anywhere alone, that's for sure. I'll do what I can to keep her occupied while we wait on you."

"I'll bet." Dawson started laughing.

"Grow up." Kaden ended the call, smiling.

He let the curtain close and pocketed his cell phone as he turned around, expecting to see Shanna waiting for him. But the room was empty. He smiled again. As long as it had taken her to shower and put her makeup on, he shouldn't be so surprised it was taking her this long to put on a pair of jeans and a blouse.

He sat on the bed, browsing through the notes she'd made this morning on her laptop. It surprised him to see a list of mines in the area, and a list of known caves around the lake. Maybe since Sam had told them the killer was calling himself the Phantom, she was looking into the legends Stella had told them about.

A few pages into her notes, he saw something else that surprised him. Questions she'd written. He read the first one.

Why didn't Kaden find Tanya's remains in the lake near the bonfire clearing?

He grimaced. He'd wondered that himself. But the water was especially deep there, and riddled with old decaying buildings and even trees that made the sonar ineffective. It was going to take a lot more dives to thoroughly search that area. He read the next notation.

KISS. Keep It Simple, Stupid.

The words were bolded and underlined. That was Shanna. She didn't pull any punches. Most of the remaining questions were typical of what they'd both been asking for days, without any answers. The last question was *Where is Jack*? Beneath that she'd written:

Tanya.
The bonfire clearing.
Jack.
Tristan. The cove.

He frowned. Did she think the killer had taken Jack to the bonfire clearing after Dawson and him had called off the boat search near there yesterday afternoon? And drowned him like he and the others had done to Tanya? It was a disturbing theory. He was really hoping that Jack would be found alive and wouldn't become another deadly Mystic Lake statistic. Hopefully, he'd be given clearance soon to search the cove again where he'd found Tristan, the one her notes mentioned. He'd use the sonar first, just in case the worst had happened and there was another fresh body down there, not buried beneath a year's worth of sediment and debris.

Jack's body.

He set the laptop aside and looked at the closed closet door. It was quiet. Too quiet. The hairs on the back of his neck stood up and a feeling of dread shot through him. He jumped to his feet and crossed the room, briefly knocking on the door before yanking it open.

The closet was empty.

Chapter Eighteen

The knife nudged Shanna in the back.

"Hurry up." The man calling himself the Phantom pushed her, making her stumble in the dark tunnel, lit only by the flashlight he was holding. "I don't like being downtown. Too many people. Don't make me cut you again, or wrap your mouth in duct tape again."

Like he'd done in the closet at the B and B. One minute she'd been pulling her shirt over her head. The next, a draft of cool, musty air had her turning to see a man coming through an opening in the wall. Before she could even scream, he'd pressed a stun gun against her neck. And before she could recover from the electrical shock, he'd shoved a cloth in her mouth and covered it with duct tape. Thankfully he'd removed it once he was far enough away from the B and B to worry about being heard. She could breathe much better without that rancid cloth in her mouth.

The sound of water dripping somewhere up ahead had her stopping. "Is—is there water down here?"

"It's a mine, in a mountain full of waterfalls and creeks. What do you think? Now, go." Once again, the knife pricked her in the back.

She jerked away from its sharp tip and forced her legs

to move, to trudge forward in spite of the panic flowing through her veins.

Drip. Drip. Drip.

Please don't let this lead to water. Don't let it be water. Please.

Finally, the tunnel began to even out, head more in what seemed like an uphill direction. She drew a relieved breath, then another. He wasn't taking her to an underground pool of water to drown her. So where was he taking her? And why?

Focus. Think.

She tried to picture the maps she'd reviewed earlier of the old, abandoned mines in the area. But the maps were from before the deadly storms had diverted the river and flooded the old town that used to be here. Were they even reliable?

Think, Shanna. Talk to him. Get the information you need.

"If—if you tell me where we're going, maybe I can go faster. It's hard to follow the path in the dark."

"Just keep going straight where my flashlight is shining. It doesn't curve again for a quarter mile. I'll tell you when to turn."

She kept going, doing her best not to stumble. She didn't want to make him mad or fall and break a bone. Staying healthy and able to run at the first opportunity was her only chance. A quarter mile to the next turn? There were only two mines she remembered on the map that were that long. The two of them had only made right turns since coming down the secret passageway at the B and B and entering this shaft. And the musty smell was still strong, The old Cooper's Bluff mine. That had to be it. The other long mine would have taken them off to the left. If they were in the Cooper's Bluff mine, then they were heading…

She started to shake. A whimper caught in her throat. She knew exactly where this mine would end.

Keep it simple, stupid.

The bonfire clearing.

Where Tanya had disappeared. Where Jack had likely disappeared. And now—now, where she would disappear.

They were heading to the lake.

"Up ahead, there's your right turn."

After making the turn, she drew several bracing breaths. How far was the bonfire clearing from here? Miles. Too far to walk. Maybe he wasn't taking her where she thought. Maybe—

"That patch of light. That's our exit."

Sunlight. The green of trees. This was her chance. She sped up.

He jerked her backward, a rock-solid arm around her neck. The cold steel of the knife pressed against her cheek. "You remember that knife back at the cabin? The one that other guy threw? He missed. I never miss. You try to take off and I'll kill you. Got it?"

"G-got it," she whispered, struggling to answer without getting cut.

He let her go, and shoved her again. She could feel the heat of him behind her as he kept close, no doubt pointing the knife at her back. She'd have to bide her time, wait for the right opportunity to escape. For now, she'd do what he said.

Kaden.

Unbidden, his image rose in her mind. What was he thinking right now? He had to have discovered that she'd gone missing. And she knew he was probably tearing the place apart searching for her. But the hidden door in the closet was locked from the other side with a thick steel bar. There was no way he'd be able to go through it even if he knew it was there. He wouldn't have any way of figuring out where she went. He didn't know about the tunnel under the B and B. According to the Phantom, no one did. But him.

She was truly on her own.

Bright sunlight temporarily blinded her as she stepped out of the mine shaft. Her captor chuckled as he jerked her arms behind her, using his duct tape again to tape them together. When her sight cleared, she realized he was wearing sunglasses. He must have put them on just before exiting the mine. She blinked and looked around. They were in the woods, in a small clearing. And on the other side of the clearing was a side-by-side, the exact same kind of four-wheeler that Sam had described.

Without a word, he lifted her onto the front passenger seat, then secured her with a seat belt. He held up the knife again, inches from her face, then chuckled and shoved it into a sheathe attached to the doorframe beside him.

"There's no one around to hear you scream, so don't bother. If you do, though, I'll gag you again so I won't have to listen to it."

"Where are we going? Why are doing this to me?"

He looked at her as if he thought she'd lost her mind. "We're kindred spirits. I'm helping you."

"Helping me?"

"Saving you from the bullies." His mouth scrunched in a sneer. "No one saved me. But I saved you. You should be thanking me for getting rid of that ex of yours."

He set the vehicle in motion, racing down a well-worn path through the woods, a path that wasn't on any of the tourist maps of the area. "They never thank me," he complained. "Not once."

They? Never? How many people had he done this to?

Practically feeling the heat of the anger seething in him, she said, "Thank you. For—for saving me."

He gave her a suspicious glance. "You're thanking me?"

"Of course." She smiled, or tried to. "Troy made my life hell. I'm sure he would have…would have hurt me if you hadn't been there. You protected me."

His chin lifted and his back straightened as if with pride. "Dang straight I did."

"Can you… Can you tell me where we're going? Please?"

His mouth curved in a benevolent smile. "I'm taking you where you've wanted to go ever since you got here and started snooping around. I'm taking you to Tanya."

Chapter Nineteen

Kaden brought the axe crashing against the Sheetrock, knocking a hole in the closet wall. Dawson immediately stepped forward, helping him break through.

"See a passageway?" Kaden asked.

Dawson shook his head. "Are you sure that Shanna didn't get past you, go out into the hallway?"

"She was in the closet. Someone's got her, that Phantom or whoever. There has to be a secret passage in the wall."

"Hey, hey, what the heck are you doing to my hotel?"

They both turned to see Stella standing in the doorway. "State police are running all over downstairs thumping on walls and now, you two are up here busting holes. What's going on?"

"He's got Shanna," Kaden told her, his voice tight and raw. "Someone took her."

"From the closet?"

"She went inside and never came out. There's a hidden door in here somewhere. Has to be."

She whirled around and left.

"Move your hands," Kaden ordered.

Dawson jumped back and Kaden brought his axe crashing down a foot to the right of the first hole. "Check it."

"Nothing. Just lumber, no gaps."

"It sounded hollow when I banged on the wall before. Maybe it's on this side."

Again, Kaden swung the axe. Again, there was no opening.

"Make room for Frank."

Kaden frowned and glanced over his shoulder. Stella ushered her husband into the tight space. He, too, was holding one of the fire axes, like the one that Kaden had grabbed from the wall in the hallway. Without a word, he shoved past Kaden and began pounding on the wall with the dull end of the axe, knocking holes as he went, in a straight line, from right to left.

Kaden swore and started doing the same thing, but from left to right. The sound of metal on metal had him whirling around.

Frank motioned toward the last hole he'd made. "Metal bar on the other side. This must be the door."

With Frank, Dawson and Kaden ripping and breaking through the Sheetrock, the passage was quickly revealed.

"Stairs," Stella announced from over their shoulders. "Well, I'll be. They go straight down. What do you think, Frank? The Cooper's Bluff mine shaft? You think it runs all the way to the B and B?"

He nodded. "Could be."

"We'll need flashlights," Kaden said.

"Hang on." Stella ran from the room.

"Dawson—"

"Yeah, yeah. I'll grab my guys from downstairs. Be right back."

Stella ran into the room, passing Dawson as he ran out. "Here, Kaden. That's the only one I could find." She gave

Frank a stern look. "Someone hasn't been keeping up with the batteries around here. The others are dead."

Frank rolled his eyes.

"Tell Dawson he'll need more flashlights," Kaden said. "I'm not waiting for him." He ducked under the metal bar that was no longer holding anything, since the Sheetrock and wood around it had been obliterated, and jogged down the steep set of steps.

Chapter Twenty

In spite of the frightening speed at which her captor raced his four-wheeler through the woods, it seemed as if they'd ridden forever until he finally began to slow. Although she'd tried to keep her bearings, to figure out where they were going, the thick canopy of trees blocked out most of the sun. It was impossible to be sure in what direction they were headed. But judging by the turns they'd made, they seemed to be going in a somewhat straight line.

That meant most likely they were still heading out of town, parallel with the lake. But where, exactly? She clenched her fists in frustration. Her one chance at escape may have been when they'd exited the mine. She should have made a run for it. Even half-blind from the sunlight she might have had a better chance than now, with her arms duct-taped behind her. He had no plans of ever letting her go. That was obvious, since he hadn't blindfolded her, as he'd done with Sam. He wasn't worried about leaving a witness behind.

Earlier she'd hoped that Kaden would find her, that he'd somehow manage to rescue her. Now, with time potentially running out, she hoped for the opposite. She prayed he wouldn't put himself in danger for her. Somehow, she'd managed to fall half-in-love with him in an incredibly short amount of time. Love at first sight? Such a cliché, but she felt it deep within her soul. She couldn't bear the thought of him getting hurt, or killed, because he tried to help her.

The vehicle finally slowed, then stopped. He grabbed his knife and pulled her out. Then he slashed her bindings as he'd done shortly after entering the mine.

She rubbed her aching wrists. "Thank you. That feels so much better."

"I only did it so you can keep your balance. I don't want to have to keep picking you up and pushing you along." He prodded her forward. "Not too much farther. You'll see."

Going as slowly as she dared, stalling for time, she tried to get more information.

"Is there something I can call you other than the Phantom? It seems so…impersonal. We're friends, right? You saved me from a bully."

He gave her a sideways look. "The Phantom is all you'll get. It's been my name for the past twenty years. No reason to change now."

"Twenty years. You've lived in Mystic Lake that whole time?"

"Mostly. Why?"

"I'm just…making conversation. Have you…saved… others? Like me?"

His eyes narrowed. "Why all the questions?"

She shrugged. "I just… I want to know more about you. You're my hero, right?" She nearly choked on the words, struggling to keep a straight face. "But I don't even know how you heard about me, or knew about Troy."

"That guy at your cabin? The one who threw a knife at you?"

"Yes."

He shrugged and jerked her arm, forcing her to move faster. "I'd heard around town about you and that boat guy looking into my business. Didn't know about this… Troy. I went to your cabin to send you a warning. I was going to leave that other bully's body as a message to tell you to keep your nose out of my business or you'd end up like him. But when I got there he was threatening you. That's when I knew what I had to do." He nodded sagely, as if his explanation made perfect sense.

"And what is that?" she asked.

He frowned and shoved her again. "Just like you said. That guy was bullying you. That's when I knew he needed to learn the lesson and that you were the one who needed saving. What are you, stupid or something?"

"I'm sorry."

He grunted and trudged along, every once in a while jerking her arm to make her go faster.

She skirted close to bushes and low hanging branches, hoping to catch some fabric on one of them as a bread crumb, a clue, for someone to find if they did come looking for her. But every time she got caught he stopped and carefully removed any trace of fabric, smiling as if he knew her game.

A few minutes later, she tried again to learn something, anything that might help her figure out what was going on and what kinds of weaknesses he might have. She needed leverage of some type if she was going to either talk her way out of this situation or plan an escape.

"Did you, ah, teach a lesson to anyone else that I might have heard of? Besides Troy. Did you teach Tristan a lesson? Jessica?"

His smug smile was his only answer. But she understood the answer as if he'd shouted at her. He'd killed both of them. Her insides ran cold. She was in the woods with a psychopath. And he'd turned his latest attentions on her.

She started to shake.

He glanced sideways at her again, not slowing. "Something wrong with you? You're shaking like you're cold. You sick or something?" He jerked her to a halt and whirled her to face him, holding up his knife. "I don't want you to get me sick. There ain't any doctors up in these mountains and most of the cabins will be filled up with tourists in the next few weeks and months. Medicine's going to be scarce and hard to find without risking being seen." He pressed the knife's tip against her throat. "Answer me. Are you sick?"

She lifted her head ever so slightly, trying to avoid the sharp blade. "No. I'm not sick. I swear. I'm just…nervous. You know, around new people."

He narrowed his eyes again as if weighing her words for truth. Then his dark eyes widened as if in understanding. And he smiled. "You're scared ain't ya? Scared of old Phil?"

"Phil? Is that your name?"

He roared with rage and slammed a fist against her jaw.

She whirled around and fell onto the ground, gnashing her teeth against the pain to keep from crying out. She didn't want to give him that satisfaction.

He stood over her and leaned down until he, and his knife, were inches from her face. "I told you my name is the Phantom."

She should have said something, begged his forgiveness. But her jaw ached and throbbed. And she was so angry she didn't think she could speak right now without telling him exactly what she thought of him. He'd probably slash her throat to shut her up. So she remained silent.

He finally straightened and stepped back. "Get up."

She was eye level with a sensitive part of his anatomy, thankfully covered by grimy jeans. She wondered if she could slam her fist against him hard enough to drop him to his knees before he could stab her.

He grabbed her arm and yanked her to her feet, then slashed the knife against her left arm, leaving a streak of red across it.

She swore and grabbed her arm.

He laughed, then sobered, pointing. "Move. We're almost there."

Hate wasn't usually in her vocabulary. But she didn't feel an ounce of remorse about hating this man right now. She marched forward, holding her throbbing arm. One benefit was that it hurt so much she barely noticed her aching jaw anymore.

A moment later, the trees seemed to fall away as they entered a clearing. She stopped so quickly he ran into her, then swore.

"I didn't tell you to stop. Move."

She stayed rooted to the spot, staring at the remains of the last bonfire that had been held here, and at the lake beyond. She'd been right after all. KISS. Keep It Simple, Stupid. Everything came back to where it had all begun, this place. Where Tanya's life had ended and the bullies who'd killed her began to disappear or die, one by one. He hadn't admitted it, but she'd heard enough, seen enough to no longer have any doubt. And if she didn't do something she was going to become his latest victim.

The water sparkled off to her right. How many times had she dived into a pool, felt the thrill of the water rushing over her, the satisfaction of well-toned muscles pulling her through it like a fish. All she had to do was run, jump in, and swim away. This Phantom—Phil—was tall and strong. But he was older than her, past middle age. And she was fast in the water, or had been. Olympic champion hopeful fast.

Go. Run. Jump.

She tried to make her legs move. But she was frozen in place. Images of the last time she'd been in the water flooded her vision. Her hair, pulling her down. Trapped. Bubbles of air escaping her lungs, rising to the surface above her. And when she couldn't hold her breath another second, the burn of chlorine spilling into her lungs as they filled with water.

Her hands fisted at her sides as she stared at the lake. But she couldn't make herself move.

He grabbed her arm, swearing when she fell. "What's wrong with you?" He grabbed her again and yanked her up, then pushed her away from the water, past the bonfire area, circling behind a large boulder.

She stopped in confusion.

"In there," he said, motioning her toward a tree in front of one of the boulders.

"I don't… What do you mean? There's nowhere to go."

He chuckled. "Sure there is. That tree is hollow. Duck down. You'll see. The cave is dark, so anyone looking at the hole in the tree won't see it. I discovered it years ago." His mouth scrunched up in a sneer. "Go on. She's waiting."

"She?"

"Tanya. You're about to join her."

He was going to kill her. Right now.

She lashed out with her foot, trying to sweep his legs out from under him.

He jumped to the side, laughing, then shoved her down and pushed her inside the hole in the tree.

She brought her hands up to protect her face from being slammed into the back of the tree. But she kept going, falling forward to the ground.

He was right. There'd been a hole in the back of the tree. She was on the cool, damp ground. A cave?

It was so dark, she could barely make out the rock walls around her. The cave dipped down, several feet below ground level. That explained why no one else had ever found it. No one would expect a large cave to be hidden behind a half-rotten tree and a boulder that was about six feet by six feet.

She sensed more than saw him standing beside her. He moved past her and she heard the sound of…keys? There was a loud click and the squeak of metal. A moment later, he was back, his hot breath making her shiver with revulsion as he leaned in close. The flashlight snapped on, startling her as it painted his face in light and shadow, like a creepy mask in a horror movie.

He laughed and aimed the light down at the sloping floor. "Shanna Hudson, meet Tanya Jericho."

She swallowed, hard, trying not to gag as he pointed the flashlight at the piles of bones that had apparently been hidden here ever since Tanya had gone missing. Except that there wasn't a pile of bones. There were metal floor-to-ceiling bars secured toward the back of the cave. And in the middle was a door, open now. That's probably the sound she'd heard earlier, his jailor's keys as he'd unlocked it. But it was what was behind that open door that had Shanna starting to shake again.

Dirty red hair, wide, frightened eyes blinking and turning away from the light. Painfully thin arms lifting to cover her eyes.

Tanya Jericho. *She was alive.*

Shanna's mouth dropped open in disbelief. Then, as if the two of them were the best of friends and had known each other for years, she ran to the other girl. They wrapped their arms around each other and held on tight, Tanya's tears quickly soaking through Shanna's shirt.

The door clanged shut behind them, startling them apart. The Phantom turned his key in the lock and chuckled. "Enjoy each other's company for a while. I'll even leave you a light." He slid the flashlight through the bars and set it on the ground. "I don't want anything to spoil this day. After all, I have big plans for Jack. Another bully will be taught a valuable lesson before the sun goes down. And don't you worry, Tanya. I'll get the others. They can't hide forever. Just ask your new friend, Shanna. I took care of her bully, too." He laughed and left the cave.

As soon as he was gone, Shanna pulled the shaking young girl down to sit on the ground. "Tanya, I can't believe it's really you. We thought you'd drowned."

"I almost did. Better if I had."

Shanna pushed the girl's hair back from her face. "Don't say that. Don't give up now. Somehow, by some miracle, you've survived for almost a year since you went missing. We're going to get out of here."

Tanya stared at her as if in shock. "A year? I've been here a whole...year?"

"You went missing almost a year ago, yes. Has he kept you here this whole time?"

She shook her head, no. "We move around. Go to cabins when it's cold or he needs to stock up. Or when he says

I stink too bad and need a shower." She grimaced. "But I always end up back here." She hung her head. "Others have been here too. I'm always happy to see them, because I'm so lonely. But then I feel guilty." Her eyes brightened with unshed tears. "He'll kill you too. Just like he's done with all the others."

Shanna stared at her in horror. "All the others? How many?"

Tanya ducked her head and shrugged, drawing her knees up and hugging them to her chest.

"Tanya?"

"Hm?"

"He's not going to kill me. And he's not going to kill you. We're going to get out of here."

Tanya sighed as if she'd heard that dozens of times and lifted her head. "Who—who are you? He made it sound like you're someone else being bullied. You're not one of the bullies?"

"I guess that's all a matter of perspective. Everyone has probably treated someone else poorly at some time in their life. Does that make them a bully? In that moment, maybe. But good people sometimes do bad things. It doesn't always mean they're bad people. Don't let that Phantom guy get into your mind, twist you to his way of thinking. Is that what he told you? That he's, what, holding you captive for your own good? That he's punishing those who hurt you?"

She shrugged. "You know about them? Peyton? Her friends?"

"Some, yes. I'm a private investigator, helping your parents find you."

Her eyes widened. "My parents? They don't think I'm dead?"

"They…haven't given up hope of finding you."

"I want to go home." The sudden longing in her voice broke Shanna's heart.

"Then let's get you home. Have you tried working any of these bars loose? They're rusty and corroded."

"The night he took me, I tried them. And for days afterward. Maybe weeks. But I gave up a long time ago."

"The night he took you? Was that at the bonfire, when the others found you watching them and got mad?"

She hung her head as if in shame. "I just thought Peyton and I could be friends if she'd give me a chance. I was watching but didn't know they saw me. They were really upset, said terrible things."

"And this man, the Phantom, he saw them?"

"He lives in the woods. He watches everyone, knows everything going on around here."

"No he doesn't."

Tanya frowned.

Shanna gave her a sad smile. "He's big and scary and I'm sure he tells you all kinds of stories to scare you, to control you. But in the end, he's just a man. We can defeat him if we work together."

Tanya shrugged noncommittally and looked away.

"Peyton told me they pushed you under the water and you never came back up. She and her friends thought they'd killed you."

"They almost did. My hair caught on something in the lake. I couldn't get away. The next thing I knew I woke up here. He—the man—he saved me from them. He got me free and brought me here to—to get justice for me, and for him, too."

Shanna stared at her, dismayed at the words tumbling

out of her mouth. She'd been brainwashed into believing the lies this Phantom told her, thinking he'd somehow saved her. But Shanna couldn't set her straight right now. All she could do was keep her talking to see whether she knew anything that could help either of them get away. She turned her attention to the bars and began twisting and pulling at them. "You said for him too. What did you mean?"

"Those bars won't come out," she said. "I've tried all of them."

"It's not like we have books to read to pass the time, right? Might as well try the bars myself," Shanna told her.

"Books." The word was uttered in awe. "I miss books."

The pain was back in Tanya's voice. Maybe there was a chance of reaching her after all, of making her realize the man who was keeping her here wasn't her savior in any way.

Shanna tugged and twisted one of the bars, wincing at the pain that shot through her cut arm. "The man who brought you here was bullied? Is that what you were telling me?"

"He was." Tanya's voice gained in strength as she regurgitated what he'd no doubt told her over and over, feeding her what he wanted her to believe. "He was bullied, just like me. They ruined his life. He couldn't…focus, keep a job."

"He's homeless."

"I guess. But it's not his fault. The kids who were mean to him in school, they're the ones who did that to him." She drew a shuddering breath. "They can't bother anyone else again. That's what he said. And he wants to do that for me, too. I told him everything I knew about Jack and the others. He made plans so they won't hurt me ever again. He's very smart."

"I'm sure he is." Shanna did her best to hide her shock.

The Phantom had apparently killed others, when he was younger. And now he was killing again. How many victims were there? She turned back to the bars, tugging and twisting harder now.

"Only Jack and Peyton are left now," Tanya said. "I think. I'm not sure about Sam, if he got him yet."

Shanna stopped and turned around to fully face her. "Got him? Tanya, did he tell you what he was going to do to each of them?"

The young girl's face twisted with despair and tears started tracking down her face. "He told me…he said he'd teach them a lesson. I said… I said…go ahead. I was angry, upset. I never expected him to actually…do what he did. When he brought Tristan here, I—"

"Tristan? Tristan Cargill?"

She nodded and wiped at her tears. "He brought him here, made him apologize to me. I told him I forgave him. Everything was okay. When he was gone, I thought… I thought the Phantom let him go. But then Jessica was here and told me Tristan…that he'd been found in the lake. It's my fault. It's all my fault." She broke down, sobbing.

Shanna held her, trying to reassure this terrorized, confused young girl. "It's not your fault. He's the one hurting people. But we can stop him, together, before he hurts anyone else. We just have to work together to get out of here. Okay?"

She hiccupped, but wouldn't meet Shanna's gaze.

Shanna sighed. She didn't have time for a therapy session. As much as she empathized with Tanya for whatever horrible things she'd suffered in the months since she'd been abducted, helping her get better was only going to happen if Shanna could get her out of this place to somewhere safe.

"We have to get out of here, Tanya. As quickly as possible."

"But there isn't any way out. Not without the keys."

"Start pulling and twisting the bars. If we can't bend or break one, we'll tunnel underneath them. We're both thin. Two, three bars would be enough. What do you say? Let's at least try. Girl power."

Tanya's lower lip trembled, but she drew a deep breath and something seemed to spark in her eyes lit by the glow of the flashlight.

Hope.

"How will we dig?" Tanya asked.

Shanna picked up the flashlight. "With this. It's made out of metal. We can use it like a shovel. But first, we have to find the weakest bars, the softest dirt. Come on. Let's do this. Let's go home."

Chapter Twenty-One

Kaden slid to a halt a short distance into the mine shaft, shining his flashlight on the ground. There were footprints in the damp earth. One set was large and deep, like a big man might make. The other was dainty and small like Shanna would make. But something was prickling at the edge of his consciousness, telling him to stop. What was it?

The map. The map of the mines from Shanna's computer. Stella had said this was the Cooper's Bluff mine shaft. That shaft went on for a good quarter mile. After that, it opened into the woods. The Phantom had a head start. And the element of surprise. He had to have reached the exit by now. Then what? Would he go through the woods? Or head to the opening of another shaft and continue underground? Where? Where to? The possibilities were endless and he could spend all day trying to find Shanna, only to arrive too late to help her.

Or he could think this through. Figure out where she was being taken. The clues were there, somewhere, niggling at him. He just had to piece them together. Fast.

In spite of his misgivings, he couldn't *not* follow. Shanna had gone this way. He couldn't just turn around and—

"Kaden," Dawson called out. "Wait up."

He turned around, holding up a hand to shield his eyes

from the flashlights as Dawson and a group of six state policemen caught up to him.

Kaden pointed to the ground. "He took her through this tunnel."

"We'll find her, sir," one of the officers said as they jogged past him.

"Why did you stop?" Dawson asked.

Shanna's notes. The last ones he'd read. What had she said? "Keep it simple, stupid."

Dawson frowned. "What?"

"Shanna's research, her notes. She knew the mines were around here. She mapped them out. And she studied the topography and…she wrote down KISS."

"Keep it simple, yeah, yeah. What of it?"

"Under that she wrote something about the bonfire clearing. No, not just something. It was specific. She wrote…" He closed his eyes, trying to picture the exact words she'd used. "Tanya. The bonfire clearing. Jack. Tristan. The cove."

"And? What does it mean?"

"I think she was saying to stop making things so complicated. The guy we're dealing with isn't some criminal mastermind. He's a thief and a coward, likely stealing people's food and supplies from the cabins in these mountains when they're empty of tourists and hunters. And for fun, or some kind of misguided sense of a divine mission, he's punishing people he believes need to be punished. Remember what Sam said the Phantom said about bullies? But this guy cheats. He doesn't fight fair. He uses a stun gun, sneaks up on them. Hell, he probably used a stun gun on Tristan to drown him. I'll bet the cuts on his bones were postmortem."

"They were. The ME confirmed it."

Kaden tightened his hand around his flashlight. “Tanya was killed at the bonfire clearing. We know that. It’s only a mile or so past Cooper’s Bluff. All the others being hurt or killed were at that clearing with her the night she went missing. That bonfire area is his comfort zone. I’ll bet he takes all his victim’s there to kill them.”

“Except Tristan. You found him on the opposite side of the lake, closer to the marina.”

“But I don’t think he was actually killed there. This guy has a pattern. Abduct someone using a stun gun. He probably uses the mines all the time to transport them where he wants to take them. He’s doing it with Shanna. Makes sense he did it with them too.”

“That’s a huge leap,” Dawson said. “We don’t know if that’s true or not. And there’s no evidence to say that Tristan wasn’t killed right where you found him. Take Jessica, for example. She was found outside the restaurant. That’s nowhere near the bonfire clearing. Is there a point to any of this speculation other than to say he’s been by Cassidy’s cabin, the restaurant, the cover, and the bonfire clearing?”

Kaden swore and raked a hand through his hair. “I’m trying to play investigator and I don’t know what the hell I’m doing.”

Dawson put his hand on his shoulder. “Take a breath. The state police are hot on Shanna’s trail. They’ll find her.”

“But will they be too late?”

Dawson remained silent.

Kaden braced a hand on the rock wall of the mine. “Think. Think. What would Shanna do if she was here? Where would she look for someone taken from the B and B down through the mine?” He straightened and turned around. “Trust her. I have to trust the work she did, her notes. Tanya. The bonfire clearing. Jack. Tristan. The cove."

"All right. We'll do it your why," Dawson said. "Trust Shanna's notes, her conclusions. She mentioned two places, right? The clearing and the cove. We can cover more ground if we split up. And we can get to both places way quicker over water than land. You drive to the Tate cabin and get your boat. Head out to the clearing. I'll take the police boat to the cove and radio my officers to split up and cover both places."

"I'm not waiting around for your team."

"I don't expect you to."

They took off running back toward the B and B.

SHANNA SWORE.

"What happened?" Tanya asked. "Are you okay?"

"I think I cut my hand. Wait. Let me get the light on again so we can see our progress."

She carefully felt for where she'd left the batteries after removing them to use the body of the flashlight as a shovel. It took several minutes of shaking the flashlight and using her shirt to wipe out the inside before the batteries got a good enough connection to flood the cave with light again.

"Definitely bleeding. But it won't kill me." She winced at her poor choice of words. "Looks, Tanya. We're getting there. Two bars dug out." But it had taken far longer than she'd hoped. "There's enough room for you to squeeze through. Go on. Hurry. Get out, run and hide before he comes back."

"Wait, leave you? No. I'll help you dig out another bar."

Shanna put her hand on the other girl's shoulder. "A lot's been happening in the past few days. He's escalating. We can't risk that he won't go ahead and kill you when he returns. Killers don't leave witnesses behind."

Tanya's eyes widened. "But I don't… I don't want to leave you behind, either."

"I'll be okay. You'll go get help, right? I need you to do that. If you don't go, we both might be trapped here, with no chance. Go. Hurry. Save us both, Tanya. Go get help."

Tanya's shoulders straightened and a determined look lit her eyes. "Help. Yes. I can do that. I'll find someone to help."

Shanna shoved at the two loose bars. Somehow, they were still attached at the top of the cave. But the bottom parts were free. She shoved them to the side so Tanya could slip through. "Now, go on. Get out of here."

"I'll—I'll come back. With help."

"I'm counting on it. Hurry."

Tanya whirled around and disappeared through the rotten tree.

Shanna braced her aching back against one of the many remaining bars. What she hadn't told Tanya was that the two bars they'd dug out were the only ones with any give at the top. She'd tried to shake and move every other bar before choosing the two they'd dug out. The rest were sunk into the boulder at the top with no movement, which meant even if she dug out more bars from the bottom, she wouldn't be able to move them to the side. And she was larger than Tanya. She couldn't squeeze through the opening the younger girl had squeezed through.

She was stuck here with no way out.

Well, there was one way. She could dig two to three feet down, so she could wiggle underneath the bars without having to swing the bars to the side. But that would take hours. The ground was hard, rocky, and her makeshift shovel was never intended for that kind of digging. Would it even last if she tried?

The only alternative was to sit here and wait for the Phantom to return. As soon as he saw that Tanya was gone, he'd know that Shanna was responsible. He'd kill her, for sure.

Which meant she no choice but to dig. And pray he didn't return anytime soon.

She took out the batteries and set them aside. Then she started to dig.

Her fingers ached from curling around the flashlight, shoving it over and over into the hard dirt. How long had she been scraping with little progress? Ten minutes? Fifteen? More? There was no way to accurately judge the time in the dark. But she couldn't stop, no matter how slow going it was. Tanya had never given up. She'd survived nearly a year in this dark hole. Shanna wasn't a quitter, either.

After shaking out the pitifully small bit of dirt she'd just scooped out, she shoved the flashlight into the dirt again.

A thump sounded from outside.

She froze, and looked toward the cave opening.

"Ladies, I brought lunch." The Phantom's cheery voice preceded him as he shoved his way through the back of the rotten tree. "Did your light go out? Here." Light filled the cave as he switched on a flashlight he was holding.

Shanna smiled. "Back so soon?"

His eyes widened. "Where is she? What have you done?"

She tightened her hold on her flashlight. "Lunch smells good. What did you bring?"

His furious shout filled the cave, echoing off the walls. He tossed the bags of food on the ground and yanked his knife out of the sheathe as he stalked toward her. "I trusted you. You've ruined everything. Now you're going to pay."

Her pulse rushed in her ears. He was going to kill her.

He shoved the key in the lock. "It's time you learned all about Mystic Lake's secrets. Let's go for a swim."

Chapter Twenty-Two

Kaden used every ounce of power the engines on his boat could give, pushing it to its limit. He recklessly passed the marina full of boaters, ignoring the shouts of anger as his wake buffeted the much smaller boats. Channel markers warned of hazards beneath the water that could shred the hull of his boat. He tried to stay away from those areas, but was forced to swerve dangerously close several times to avoid decimating small boats that couldn't get out of his way fast enough.

Still, he pushed for more horsepower.

The mist was still mysteriously hovering over the lake, making it even harder to watch out for potential hazards. But what frustrated him the most was that the mist seemed heaviest at the water's edge. He couldn't see the shoreline to judge exactly where the lake ended and the shore began. If, by some miracle, Shanna was on the shore, perhaps running from her abductor, he wasn't even sure that he would see her.

Forced to rely on his training and experience, he used the boat's instrumentation and the GPS coordinates from his earlier search of the bonfire area to navigate. He was close. Very close. He powered down three of the four engines and dramatically decreased his speed all at once, making the boat rock back and forth like a toy in a bathtub. It creaked and groaned but quickly settled.

According to the GPS, he was fifty yards from shore. The bonfire clearing could be up ahead, in front of those trees, but the mist was too thick for him to be sure.

"Shanna," he yelled, even as he edged the boat dangerously closer. "Shanna!"

A figure appeared, the mist swirling around her. A woman near the tree line. But she was too short to be Shanna. Red hair glinted in the sunlight. What the… Was that *Tanya*?

She jumped up and down, waving her arms. "Help! Help! He's going to kill her. Help!"

Kaden's shock at seeing the young girl alive quickly gave way to dread. He shoved a lever, revving the engine again, rapidly closing the distance. The mist thinned, revealing he was much closer to the shoreline than he'd realized. He turned hard to starboard just in time to turn the boat and avoid grounding it, then returned the engine to idle, bobbing up and down in his own wake.

He stepped out of the wheelhouse and leaned against the railing. "Tanya Jericho?"

"Yes, yes. Please, you have to help her. Shanna. He's got her. I tried to go find help. But he got there too fast. I had to hide. I saw him take her out of the rock."

Rock? He had no idea what she meant. "Where is she?" he yelled across to her.

"There. Over there. He said he was taking her for a swim." She pointed off to her left, Kaden's right.

A swim? Oh, God, no.

"How far?" he yelled.

"Around the next curve."

"Hide, Tanya. Don't come out until you see the police."

She waved in understanding and sprinted into the trees.

Kaden jumped back in the wheel house and gunned the engine again, sending the boat in a full out frenzy parallel to the shore toward the next bend. Another debris marker appeared out of the mist directly in front of him. He swore and jerked the wheel away from the shore. Something hard made a sickening scrape against the hull, but it didn't catch. The boat shot out past it into deeper, safer water.

He quickly turned, powering down again and heading around the next curve where Tanya had said Shanna would be. So where was she?

He scanned the area, swearing as the mist rose thick again, covering the surface of the water. Then he heard it. Splashing.

The mist suddenly opened in front of him like a red carpet rolling out to guide his way. And there, to his horror, in the shallow strip of land at the lake's edge was Shanna with her captor. He had her by the hair and was shoving her under the water.

The gun Dawson had given Kaden was useless. He'd likely hit Shanna if he tried shooting the Phantom. But Kaden had another weapon. *Discovery.* He throttled up, hurtling the boat directly toward shore.

The Phantom looked up, as if just noticing him. He stared at Kaden, smiling as he held a thrashing Shanna under, seemingly convinced Kaden wouldn't hit him.

Kaden gave the engine another burst of speed.

The Phantom shoved Shanna completely under water and scrambled to his feet, desperately trying to get out of Kaden's way.

Kaden jerked the wheel hard to starboard to miss where

he'd last seen Shanna. He ran to the port side, grabbing his handheld sonar as he dove into the water. A loud explosion sounded overhead as his boat ran aground and struck the trees. A concussion of power slammed against his body, tossing him against something hard and unyielding. The impact knocked the breath out of him but he managed to maintain his grip on the sonar device.

He struggled against the urge to suck in water as his lungs screamed for air. Pieces of his boat fell into the water, like a hard rain. Then he was kicking for the surface.

He sucked in a lungful of air, then dove back down, immediately sweeping the sonar back and forth. In what felt like minutes, but was probably only a few seconds, one of the lights came on, pointing him toward a shadow several feet below.

Shanna.

Diving straight down, he found her. Her eyes were open and staring. But she didn't see him. His heart seemed to stop in his chest. He tossed the device aside, grabbed her and swam for the surface, but pulled up short. Her hair was wrapped around an old wooden railing of a submerged house.

He savagely kicked the railing, smashing it in two, freeing her. Cradling her lifeless body against him, he headed for the surface as fast as he could go. Once he reached the shore, he laid her on her side and worked to pump the water out of her lungs. A rush of water came out but she didn't cough or start breathing. He rolled her onto her back and began CPR.

"Come on, Shanna. Don't you leave me now, not after becoming everything to me. Don't you dare. Breathe, damn it. Breathe."

He blew two quick hard breaths, watching her chest rise as her lungs filled with air. But just like with Jessica, she didn't breathe on her own. And this time, there wasn't an external defibrillator to help him. He desperately pressed his clasped hands over her heart, pumping it for her, and praying harder than he'd ever prayed in his life.

Please, God. Please. Don't take her. Let her live. Please.

An angry shout was his only warning. He threw up his arm to deflect the blow as the Phantom swung a piece of broken wood from his boat down toward his head. Kaden kicked out at the other man, catching him in the groin.

As the Phantom fell to his knees, cupping himself and groaning in agony, Kaden blew two quick breaths into Shanna's lungs. Still nothing. "Come on, sweetheart. Come on. Don't leave me." He started compressions again.

The Phantom struggled to his feet, glaring at Kaden. His mouth turned up in a feral grin as he slowly pulled out a long, wicked knife.

This was it. He'd probably end up sinking that knife into Kaden. But if he stopped compressions long enough to fight him off, Shanna didn't stand a chance. He had to keep going as long as he could.

Where the hell was Dawson's team?

As if in answer, the distant sound of a boat engine whined out across the lake.

Thank God. His boat disintegrating into a million pieces must have alerted them.

"I love you, Shanna," he whispered, before blowing two more quick breaths.

The Phantom drew his knife above his head and let out the sound a rabid dog might make as he limped forward, still cupping himself with his other hand.

Kaden continued compressions, turning his back to protect Shanna from the coming blow.

The mist suddenly swirled around them, thick and impossible to see through.

The sound of the Phantom's footsteps faltered as he seemed to struggle to search for his prey.

Kaden took advantage of the opportunity, grabbing Shanna in his arms and charging forward to the cover of the trees. He dropped down with her and immediately continued compressions.

And just as suddenly as the mist had come, it disappeared. Kaden glanced through the trees toward the shore.

The Phantom turned his way, spotting him. His face contorted with a victorious smile as he held the blade of his knife and raised it to throw it.

A hail of gunfire sounded from the lake. There, on the small police boat, to Kaden's surprise, was Dawson himself. He held a rifle aimed at the Phantom.

The Phantom's smile turned to dismay and shock as he looked down at the holes in his chest. He staggered toward the lake, then fell facedown into the water, disappearing beneath its murky surface into the depths below.

The sound of a cough had Kaden jerking his head toward Shanna and stopping the compressions. She blinked up at him, her beautiful blue eyes glassy, unfocused.

"Shanna? It's Kaden. Can you hear me?"

Her eyes closed and her head lolled to the side, water trickling out of her mouth.

He swore and turned her, moving her arms to try to clear more water from her lungs. When he rolled her on her back, his panic gave way to relief when he saw that she was breathing. But her pulse was thready, far too weak. And all he could think about was how he'd revived Jessica and she still hadn't survived.

"Don't you dare die on me," he ordered, his voice breaking. "I swear I'll never forgive you."

Her brow wrinkled as if she'd heard him. But her eyes stayed closed.

He lifted her in his arms, cradling her against his chest as he staggered to his feet. Then he was running toward the lake to where Dawson was now idling his boat dangerously close to the shoreline. A body bag on the deck told Kaden what he'd feared might happen. Dawson must have found Jack. But he'd been too late.

Dawson's eyes widened. "Is she—"

"She's alive," Kaden said. "But she's in bad shape. Get the chopper out here. Now."

Chapter Twenty-Three

Kaden stood in his suit outside the hospital behind the others at the makeshift memorial, a tiny plaque shoved into the dirt in front of a sapling that would eventually grow into a mighty oak tree. It was a simple gesture, but heartfelt. If nothing else, it helped everyone here feel as if they'd honored her memory.

He'd have traded it in a second to have been able to save her.

As the small crowd of doctors and nurses began to disperse, he glanced off to his left at some of those who remained. Her family was here, of course. Tanya, surprisingly, was here too, in a wheelchair, just beginning her long road to recovery. Her mother was clucking around her like a worried hen. Beside her, Cassidy Tate, sporting a tan from her recent cruise, fussed over Tanya just as much as her mother. Behind the wheelchair, Tanya's father couldn't stop smiling.

A wave caught Kaden's attention. Chief Dawson stood at the outer fringe, away from the others, waving goodbye. Kaden returned the gesture and Dawson headed toward the parking lot.

He was going through as much guilt as Kaden, maybe more. The deaths of so many young people in his town at the hands of the Phantom weighed heavily on the police chief whose job was to protect them. No amount of commiseration from Kaden had done anything to make Dawson even begin to forgive himself.

Kaden sighed heavily. Those feelings would only get worse in the coming days and weeks as more of the Phantom's sins were revealed. Tanya was only just beginning to open up to a therapist and reveal the confessions that Phil Gunther—the Phantom's real name—had made to her. Many of the drownings and disappearances throughout the years that had been blamed on Mystic Lake's hazards or some ethereal ghost had actually come at the hands of one bitter, deranged man who'd been bullied one too many times and had decided to take his revenge.

"I'm sorry about your boat," a feminine voice called out from behind him.

He gave one last look at the plaque for Jessica DeWalt and turned around, smiling at the beautiful woman staring up at him from her wheelchair.

Shanna.

He nodded his thanks to Gavin Tate, who'd surprised him by wheeling her out here. Gavin squeezed Shanna's shoulder, then headed toward his wife who was still fussing over Tanya.

"Boats can be replaced," Kaden told her. "You can't."

"Neither can you. And you almost got yourself killed for me."

"Worth it."

She frowned. "Not worth it. I don't want you dying for me." She leaned toward him as if to try to stand, then winced and eased back. "Stupid ribs. They're so dang sore."

He crouched in front of her. "I'm so sorry. Apparently I need better CPR training. I seem to hurt anyone I try to help."

She shook her head. "Don't you dare apologize. You've done nothing but apologize since I woke up in this hospital. You have nothing to be sorry about. You saved me."

He winced. "That honor goes to Chief Dawson. He's the one who shot the Phantom."

"Who would have already drowned me if you hadn't come along. Dawson merely dealt the final blow. Or, at least, I hope it was final. Have they found the body yet?"

"Not yet. My team's arriving tomorrow morning with another sonar device, and another boat, to search that part of the lake. They won't leave until they find him. The town has suffered enough because of the rumors and myths about the lake. The Phantom has to be found so everyone can truly relax and feel safe again.

"Phil Gunther." She shook her head. "He was a local after all. Or, at least, he started out that way. Cassidy showed me his picture in a yearbook from the school library. He grew up here, graduated from the same school as Peyton and the others. Then he spent the rest of his life stalking and killing. He lived off the mountains, sneaking around essentially unseen to listen in on people's conversations in town, staying one step ahead of the law. I still can't believe it." She glanced at the group of family and friends surrounding Tanya. "Or believe that we actually found Tanya alive."

Her eyes turned misty. "Eleven months of captivity. Torture. She hasn't begun to scratch the surface and tell everyone everything she suffered. If only I'd agreed to help in the beginning, when Cassidy first called—"

"Don't." He feathered a hand down the side of her beautiful face. "You don't know whether you could have helped back then, whether things would have fallen into place like they did for you and me. You might have investigated and given up, thinking she'd drowned. You coming here when you did, at the same time as me, was fate. She might never have been found otherwise."

She wiped at her eyes. "That's one way to look at it, I suppose."

"The only way."

She didn't appear to be convinced, but offered him a small nod. "I haven't heard any updates on Peyton. She has to feel awful with so many of her friends…gone. But knowing she didn't kill Tanya has to help. I suppose."

"I hear she and Sam have been seen together in town since Dawson let her out of protective custody and Tanya refused to press any charges against her. Maybe Peyton and Sam will help each other through the fallout and become better people for it."

"I hope so." She stared at him a long moment, her gaze searching his. "We've talked about everyone else but us. What…what are your plans? You've stayed well past your original plan. I imagine things are piling up at your company."

She drew a shaky breath, as if to hold back tears and turned away.

He gently pressed his hand beneath her chin until she looked at him again. "I'm not going anywhere. Not without you."

She blinked. "I don't…what do you mean?"

"I love you, Shanna Hudson."

Her eyes widened. Her throat worked but no words came out.

He hoped that was a good sign.

Straightening, he pulled the small box out of his pocket that he'd been carrying around since the moment she'd awakened in the hospital and had been declared out of danger. Then he dropped to one knee in front of her wheelchair.

"Oh, my God," she whispered, staring at him. "Kaden? What are you doing?"

"Solving our long-distance-relationship problem." He flipped open the black velvet box and pulled out the diamond solitaire ring sitting there.

For once, Shanna seemed shocked into silence.

"Shanna Hudson, will you do me the honor of becoming my wife?"

She stared at the ring, then at him. "Kaden, we haven't even known each other for a whole month!"

"And in that time we've been together almost twenty-four seven. I've done the math. We've known each other longer than if we'd just casually dated a few times a week for well over a year."

She burst out laughing. "I'm not sure about your math, but that's a pretty clever argument."

"Is that a yes?"

Her smile faded. "Where would we live? We both have businesses a full day's drive from each other."

"We're both entrepreneurs. And young enough to start over. I can sell my company to my team. They'd love to all have part ownership in it. You could do the same with yours, if you want. We can start our own business together, or retire early on our profits from the sales. I'm not exactly hurting, financially. I've got quite a nest egg saved up. We can go anywhere you want to go. I'll even live in West Virginia if that's where you prefer to be, at the top of the tallest mountain." He searched her gaze. "That is, if I've read you right. I told you I loved you. Now it's your turn. Unless… I'm completely wrong here?"

"Oh, Kaden. How could I not love you?"

Joy and relief swept through him. "One down. One to go. What about my other question?"

She stared at him in amazement. "You're willing to brave driving up a scary mountain road for me? And live at the very top?"

"I'm willing to brave anything if you say yes."

She laughed and held out her hand. "Yes, yes, yes!"

He slid the ring on her finger, then kissed her, far more gently than he wanted, careful not to hurt her cracked ribs. When he pulled back, tears were tracking down her face.

"Happy tears," she assured him. "I love you, Kaden Rafferty. And I want nothing more than to spend the rest of my life showing you." She gave him a sexy wink.

He was grinning so hard his mouth hurt. He jumped to his feet and turned her wheelchair around, then pushed her toward the hospital, racing across the concrete.

"Whoa, horsey," she called out. "Why the rush? Slow down?"

"We have to see the doctor. Right now."

She looked up at him. "Why? What's wrong?"

"I'm going to bribe him to spring you out of here so we can get started on you showing me how much you love me." He gave her a sexy leer.

She burst out laughing and pointed to the hospital doors. "Onward, my prince. Our forever is waiting."

* * * * *